DANGEROUS RESPONSIBILITIES

DANGEROUS RESPONSIBILITIES

PIERCING THE VEIL™ BOOK TWO

RENÉE JAGGÉR

MICHAEL ANDERLE

DON'T MISS OUR NEW RELEASES

Join the LMBPN email list to be notified of new releases and special promotions (which happen often) by following this link:

http://lmbpn.com/email/

LMBPN Publishing
PMB 196, 2540 South Maryland Pkwy
Las Vegas, NV 89109

Version 1.00, April 2023
eBook ISBN: 979-8-88878-178-4
Print ISBN: 979-8-88878-179-1

THE DANGEROUS RESPONSIBILITIES
TEAM

Thanks to our Beta Readers:
Kelly O'Donnell, Malyssa Brannon, David Laughlin,
Angela Wood

Thanks to the JIT Readers

Dave Hicks
Dorothy Lloyd
Christopher Gilliard
Diane L. Smith
Zacc Pelter
Jan Hunnicutt

If we've missed anyone, please let us know!

Editor
SkyFyre Editing Team

CHAPTER ONE

Natalie looked up from her computer and watched Rich at a desk with Lucas, leaning over the AR glasses the three of them had built together.

Lucas was their hardware guy. The one problem was that Lucas had been turned into a cat. A cursed cat. And he was losing more and more of himself.

"Not like that," Lucas insisted for about the eighth time in the past twenty minutes.

Rich exhaled as if he wanted to throw it across the room.

"I know it's not easy. You need steady hands and to know exactly what you're doing." Lucas spoke as clearly as he could, but he was sounding more catlike than before. At first, his words had been clear and he'd sounded like his normal self. But as the days passed, he had become more and more like a tabby cat.

It was heartbreaking, but they were all trying not to dwell on it.

In the other corner of the room sat Alia, a young elf

who lived a life of thievery within a code of her own making. It was something the three of them had come to terms with when they'd decided to live with her. She'd been cleared of her past by the enforcers in the magical world when they'd defeated a magical wizard and stopped him from using the Santa myth to take over the whole world.

They had gone up against the wizard to get Lucas back. It hadn't succeeded, and now the wizard was dead and all the slaves making goods in his warehouse had been freed. Unfortunately, every curse he'd cast, including turning Lucas into a cat, had stuck when he died.

Alia was sitting with a magic tabloid on her lap, scanning through the articles and information in an attempt to find them some work or something that could help Lucas.

In the meantime, they were trying to figure out what to do with the AR glasses they had created. It had meant to be a system that showed the world with a fantastical overlay, shifting how everything looked and making the world pretty, and it did that. Trees and animals looked different.

That wasn't all it did, though.

The glasses also showed a magical element to the world that the average human was oblivious too. Werewolf packs, elves, and all sorts of other magical data was pulled from some database that the glasses had hooked into.

It was a fluke that they could see it, and it had led them on a whirlwind of an adventure in the week or so since. But now the glasses were slightly broken, and Lucas was trying to walk Rich through fixing them.

Natalie was left with the unenviable task of talking to all the potential investors and folks who had donated cash at points in the last few months to work out what was going to happen. Selling the glasses and the technology behind them had always been their goal, but now they weren't so sure.

It would put the fantastical races they had discovered in danger in multiple ways, and they had discovered that the magical world was dangerous for humans, too. The average person who bought these glasses was either going to cause a lot of trouble for the magical realm or get themselves in a lot of trouble.

But all that meant telling the investors something else. Because they couldn't afford to give the investors back their money. Not right now anyway.

She picked up the phone and wandered to another room of the house to take a call.

"Hi, Mr. Jacobs."

"Natalie, I was hoping to talk to you. How is your little project coming along? I understand that it's past when you were hoping to deliver a prototype."

"We're really close now, sir." She was careful to be extra polite. "We've got something that sort of works. Not exactly the way intended, but we're getting closer. Sadly, our hardware guy, Lucas, has come down with a really nasty illness. One of those ones where we just have to let it run its course and let him recover gently."

"I'm sorry to hear that. Send him my best wishes for a speedy recovery."

"Thank you. I'm sure he'll be grateful for that. He's really struggling with having good spirits. The project means so much to him and he feels so close to having it the way he wants it."

"What does it mean for the project?"

Natalie had rehearsed this answer. "We're eager to keep going, but we have to balance encouraging Lucas to rest. I am confident it's only going to delay us."

"I'm glad to hear it. I'm very anxious to see what you three come up with. If you're close and you have something working, at least a little, perhaps we could have a demonstration in a couple of weeks anyway?"

"I wouldn't be able to commit to something like that without talking to Lucas first and being sure he's well enough to do so. With the prototype and the current system, it would really need to be him who shows you what it's currently capable of." Her heart was racing at having to lie so much and try to make it sound natural.

"Of course, I understand. Keep me informed and I hope Lucas is better soon."

Natalie hung up and waited a moment for her breath to calm down. She only needed to do the same thing another five times.

She'd started with their biggest investor, but he was also the most understanding. It was going to get harder from here on out.

Before Natalie could summon up the energy to tackle calling another of the investors and run the gauntlet of questions for a second time, there was a knock on the front door.

Everyone froze. They were staying in an Unplace where Alia had a small house. It was meant to be a temporary arrangement, as the young elf was technically squatting, but they could lie low while they got themselves sorted. No one knew where they were or how to find them.

Alia got up and went to the door as Natalie, Rich, and Lucas tucked themselves up and out of the way. She tried to look through the glass to the side to get an idea of what to expect before she opened the door.

The voice of an enforcer came through the closed door. "Alia, open up. We know you and your friends are in there. We're not here to kick you out or arrest you for anything. We want to talk to you about some recent events."

Alia glanced at the trio to be sure they were okay with her opening the door. Natalie was scared about what they wanted, but if they knew Alia and the others were inside the building, there wasn't much they could do about it.

The elf opened the door to reveal two enforcers and the car in the background that they'd got in with.

"How did you find me?" she asked as she stepped back and let the two men in.

"It took us a while. We'll admit that much. But eventually, a little persuasion had someone saying they'd seen you drive a sleigh into an Unplace near here. And we all know how to find an Unplace when we know there's one to be found."

"All right, so why did the pair of you want to find us?" she asked. "We've been here quietly, letting people bring us food and thank us and getting on with figuring out how to make an honest living now Daven is gone."

"And figure out how to get Lucas turned back into a human," Natalie stepped forward to remind them. Annoyance made her seem braver than she was.

The enforcers looked her way, but they didn't take the hint and acknowledge that they were meant to be doing something about it.

"Honestly, it's a little complicated. Do you think you could all sit down and let us explain? We might need your help with something."

The enforcers motioned to the chairs and sat on the sofa side by side. They looked out of place in the small room, and it meant that Natalie had to perch on the arm of the chair Alia sank into. Rich stayed in the desk chair with the glasses on the surface beside him, and Lucas sat on the desk.

"We've been struggling with this werewolf—"

Alia held up her hand to interrupt the men.

"If you two are going to come in here and ask for our help, I want names. Who are the pair of you and what makes you think I'll want to help you when you've spent years making my life harder when I was only ever trying to survive."

"I'm Jason, and this is Lincoln. We're sorry that we've clashed with you in the past. Often we have just been following protocol. No magic items used without the proper care, attention, and in some cases permits."

"Sounds like you've been interpreting the phrase 'proper care' how you want to so you can throw your weight around," Natalie pointed out as she folded her arms across her chest.

The enforcers looked at each other, and for a moment Natalie wondered if she'd put them off asking for assistance. It might be a good idea to help them. It could make them more amenable to helping save Lucas.

"Look, we really came here because we know you have those glasses. And we're sure that the three of you don't mean trouble. But you do still have some tech that could make some very important people feel threatened. Keeping them happy is in all of our best interests."

It was a good point and Alia only had to glance at Rich and Natalie for them to see that they were all in agreement.

"You mentioned a werewolf, Lincoln?" Alia asked.

"Yes. A con artist, to borrow the phrase. He's been tricking people into all sorts of things, and we think we've finally got him for something, but he's gone to ground. He's hidden himself from us in multiple disguises and none of it is magic. There just isn't any way for us to find him very easily."

"What can we do to help?" Natalie frowned, leaning closer as Lincoln got out his phone and pulled up a picture of this guy.

"It comes down to those special glasses of yours. Assuming you still have them and they do truly work the way you say that they do, then they should be able to find him. No matter what he's wearing, the database should be able to work out if it's him or not."

Stunned silence followed this statement. Were law enforcement officials asking them to use their AR glasses to help them solve a case? It seemed more than a little insane.

CHAPTER TWO

"What's in it for us?" Alia asked when she finished contemplating the request the two enforcers had tabled.

"Uhhh…" Jason looked at Lincoln as if this was something he wasn't expecting or hadn't thought that he might be asked. It annoyed Alia more. Surely the enforcers knew that she didn't risk anything for anyone without at least some hope of financial reward?

"We're going to need more than his race," Rich warned. He frowned a moment later. "Assuming 'werewolf' is a race."

Lincoln blinked a few times before he nodded. He held up several pictures showing a tall, lithe man, with a muscular body and a glint in his eyes.

"This is him in human form. Francisco. He spends almost all of his time in the affluent parts of the city among magical folk and he charms his way from place to place. But he's nothing but a thief. Someone who gets people hooked on something he's selling and then he does the dirty and takes them for all he can."

"Sounds like a nice guy," Alia held out her hand to get a better look at the picture. "Where do you think he is now?"

"Lying low somewhere." Lincoln handed her the phone and she held it up for everyone else to see.

Natalie's eyes went wide as she stared at the guy. "Wow. Does he work out or something?"

Alia chuckled at Natalie's reaction. "He's a werewolf. He's a predator to your kind. Just like vampires, they're designed to appear attractive to anyone who might make good prey."

Natalie shuddered, but that didn't stop her from ogling him.

It was something that never worked on Alia. She was naturally untrusting enough that she saw past the glamour and the false charm and saw it for what it was: a genetic trick that was caused by the race's natural predatory advantages. That wasn't something all elves had. She was one of only a few who could feel like that and not be taken in.

Most of the time, however, the werewolves followed the rules like everyone else did. Everyone did, because everyone knew it was better for the human world not to know anything about them. At least, that's what they all told themselves.

"What makes you think that we'll want to help you on this?" Rich asked. "You still haven't said anything other than *you* need *us*. While I don't mind being a good citizen now and then, with no idea of the risk or the reward, I think that it's asking a lot."

"There is a financial reward," Lincoln finally allowed. "I

know that you're all struggling for work and we know you don't have the right to live here."

Alia bristled. "I hope that you're not threatening to have me kicked out if I don't help you? Cause if you are, you should know by now that something like that will only make me less likely to help you."

"The glasses might help us find him," Natalie broke in to change the subject. "I certainly don't think I'd mind looking for him."

She grinned as she looked him over again.

Alia smothered a laugh. Although she'd never say it out loud or give any outward indication, she saw the appeal of the werewolf.

"Does this mean that you'll do it?" Lincoln pressed.

"I don't think we can," Rich replied. "Lucas needs our focus. Unless you've managed to find anything that will break the curse upon him and return him to human form."

"Curses always break upon the death of the person who cast it."

"If that were true then Lucas would be human again. And look." Alia pointed at the tabby cat sitting on the table.

"That's a cat." Jason looked at Lucas as if that settled the matter.

"I'm not a cat. At least not normally." Lucas kept his voice even and sounded almost bored.

The two enforcers didn't seem to know what to say in response.

Alia got up, put her hand on her hip, and moved to Lucas' side. "Have you found anything at all? Even looked into it? We asked if we could have some of the books from the library."

"In an active investigation, it's not possible for the evidence to be used for any other purpose. We cannot do anything further to help you when we are assigned to investigate this new case. Will you help us? Maybe then there would be something that we could do."

Alia growled, unable to believe the cheek of these two men, but it wasn't completely up to her. The glasses were the creation of the other three, and Lucas was one of them. She wouldn't have given in and helped the enforcers, but it wasn't her friend at risk and she didn't get to decide what to do with the tech.

At the end of it all, she also knew that whatever they decided, she would support them. They had been there for her and had used their good fortune to support Alia. They hadn't judged her for her past and they'd given her respect for surviving how she'd needed to.

After everything she had been through, it was the first time she didn't feel alone. She would have their back.

"I understand that you're in a difficult position," Natalie replied. "But so are we. We're losing our friend, and as much as we want to help you, we can't change our course and we definitely can't afford to waste the time needed to save him. There's possibly information in those books that can help us save a man's life. Whatever you could do to help us would be appreciated."

Lincoln gulped at Natalie's passionate plea and Alia wondered if it just might work. Everyone waited for the enforcers to either give in to the request or work through the implied guilt Natalie had dished out.

"We can try and help, but breaking a curse is something that is normally only guaranteed by a death."

"Well, unless you want to resurrect Daven Hoth and let us kill him for a second time… that's not going to be an option." Alia folded her arms across her chest.

The enforcers exhaled, glanced at each other again, and, as if they shared one mind, got to their feet.

"We hope that you can find what you need. We understand that you have to do what is important to you, but I want to add that there is a reward for catching this criminal and getting him to face justice. A very sizable reward. He really has hurt a lot of very wealthy people."

Alia noticed that they emphasized a few words to make it clear that they wanted Rich and Natalie to consider the money as well. It wasn't going to work. Even if they had been more desperate for the cash, they had good hearts. They weren't the sort of people to be mercenaries, even when they needed to be.

While Lucas was in danger and needed their help he would be their priority. Alia liked that about these guys.

"Thank you, but the answer is still no. Good luck with your investigation." Natalie went to the door and opened it, making it clear that the two enforcers were no longer welcome. They backed out of the room, nodding as they did.

Near the door, Lincoln pulled a business card from his pocket and handed it to Natalie.

"I really hope that you get your friend back and I'll see what we can do to help. If you do manage to work on anything for us or feel you have the time, drop me a call and I'll go over the details and any questions you might have."

"If we look into it, you'll be the first to know." She opened the door wider.

They got the message.

"Anyone else think that was almost creepy and definitely really intimidating?" Natalie asked when she'd closed the door.

"It was irritating," Rich replied. "They want to abuse our technology already, but they don't want to help us in return. That's pretty shitty of them."

"I don't know, it seemed like their hands were tied." Natalie frowned and bit her lower lip.

"They would all love to give the excuse that their hands are tied," Alia pointed out. "It means they don't have to do anything. But the money might be useful. Let's prioritize finding a cure for Lucas, and if we find that helping them can be done on the side, let's do both."

Silence followed Alia's proposal. It wasn't a bad idea and it meant they didn't have to give up the money necessarily. It was enough for now.

CHAPTER THREE

It took everyone a little while to settle, but eventually they went back to what they had been doing. Lucas tried to explain to Rich how to fix the glasses again. Natalie resumed calling their investors to put them off asking for their money back or demanding to see a product.

Over the last week or so, Alia had exhausted every avenue she could think of to find a cure for Lucas, and she'd discovered others who were also cursed. Now she was at a standstill and had one course of action open to her. She pulled open her laptop and searched for the werewolf Francisco.

The magical community was careful about what they had on the net and where, so it took her a while to find anything on him, but she knew where to look and found him in the end.

She had to hack around a bit and ask in some shady forums on the dark web for a little assistance, but by the time Rich was well underway fixing the glasses and Natalie had done all her calls, Alia had begun to build a decent picture of where this werewolf had come from and what crimes he was committing.

Natalie huffed as she sat beside Alia and looked over at what she was doing.

"Still annoyed at the enforcers?" Alia asked as she skimmed more of the information.

"Very. But not them entirely. It's…"

"Complicated."

"Isn't it always?"

Alia chuckled.

"I just don't get why everyone keeps telling us that it's impossible. If curses can be broken then there's got to be a way to break this curse. Lucas is still in there."

Rich looked up from his soldering. "They're only saying it's impossible because they're in over their heads. To them it *is* impossible."

"Then why don't they say that to us?" Natalie demanded. "Why not tell us that it's not something they know about or that they don't understand it either? Instead of telling us we need to kill an already dead guy?"

"Sometimes people can't cope with finding out that everything they thought they knew about magic is wrong," Alia suggested as she tapped at the keys. "There. I've got what we need."

Lucas jumped up on the table beside her laptop as Natalie leaned in closer. Rich stayed where he was and continued working.

Natalie ogled the open-shirted picture of him walking off a large yacht. "Wow, he really is hot, isn't he?" There were several other people in the photo with him. In this case, it was one of his wealthy marks and someone who had been conned out of the boat they were pictured on.

It had been a stupid con because it wouldn't have been easy to re-sell a boat so obviously belonging to someone rich, but somehow Francisco had done so and got away with it.

"It says here that he not only got the boat assigned to him but that he sold it in such a way that when the original owner went to buy another, the first one they were offered was their own yacht."

Rich winced. "Ouch, that's gotta hurt the ego." He never looked up from his tinkering, engrossed in the work despite his comments.

"So he's rich too?" Natalie asked.

"Stop drooling. He's got to be bad news," Lucas snapped. "Someone like that could never be trusted with anything."

It was a sad truth, and Alia nodded.

"He's right. Werewolves in general can be very shady characters. I'm not going to stereotype them because there are some lovely packs in the city and I've worked with a few I adore in the past," Alia explained. She sat back to focus on Natalie. "In general, though, it's better to be wary of them. Especially for a human."

"It sounds like humans should be wary of every fantastical race for one reason or another," Natalie reminded her.

"In some ways, this is true. But you can learn enough to not have to fear the vast majority. You're just at a disadvantage to begin with."

"Well, I don't think we're going anywhere anytime soon. And Lucas needs us to save him, so let's get started.

Teach us what we need to know about this Francisco and werewolves in general."

Alia grinned and moved back to the laptop. After pulling up more information on werewolves in general, Alia explained that they often lived in packs. They were interesting people to learn about and reminded Natalie of some of the things people had told her about the mafia and its family dynamic. Instead of having everyone in a direct family be a mafia unit allied with other families, they had packs and a set of werewolves or a single werewolf that led that pack.

To Natalie's surprise, not all the packs were led by a male werewolf—more than a quarter were led by strong and respected women. Alia brought no attention to it or didn't think it worthy of mentioning, and Natalie got the impression that this was normal and that the werewolves weren't suddenly doing something special.

"They don't sound too bad," Lucas added when Alia paused.

"When they get angry they can get...really angry. And others can be caught up in the crossfire when they fight. They also don't suffer fools gladly. They've been known to outcast their own kind for not being strong enough, or appearing to be too dumb."

"That sounds a bit mean."

"They don't tolerate a lot of weakness in general. Which is where our Francisco comes in. He's a werewolf without a direct pack. He was outcast from his original pack and although he's now built himself up into something better and stronger, he has refused to join a different pack."

"He's the typical lone wolf."

"Pretty much. He'll work with other packs, and he has friends, but he does a lot of his cons by himself and he often travels alone. No mate either."

Natalie sighed and Alia rolled her eyes.

"You really shouldn't pay him any attention," Alia added.

"I know. I can swoon now and be over it by the time we'd ever cross paths with him." Natalie grinned, and Alia felt better. Broken hearts weren't fun, and it sounded as if this werewolf was smooth. She didn't want to see Natalie get hurt.

"Okay, so do we know what he's wanted for, or are we going to need to phone those two goons back and listen to them tell us, yet again, that they don't know much and can't help us break the curse on Lucas?" Rich asked. He had finished sorting what he was fixing and was reassembling the glasses again.

"Let me find out." Alia tapped away again. "I don't want to ask those two anything either, but it might be difficult to get his enforcer records without doing it. I might know a person, though."

"How dangerous is it to hack something the magical government controls? Like the enforcer system?" Rich asked.

She blinked, surprised. After thinking a moment, she responded, "I reckon we could do that. Might take a little work, but do you think you're capable of actually doing something like that?"

Natalie's smile grew wider and she motioned for Alia to scoot over so she could type. Alia acquiesced and let her try to hack the system.

It took longer than Alia expected it would, but Natalie navigated through the system until she had a screen showing the search function for files on current crimes.

Natalie relinquished the computer and Alia took back over. "Wow, that is so cool."

Within seconds she was searching for everything about Francisco. She found a lot, including some suspected crimes that weren't directly attributed, all of them at least partially unsolved. It seemed that proving this guy had done anything wrong was the biggest challenge in most cases, but he was also hard to pin down. He was a master of disguise and wealthy enough to have a private jet that left the enforcers struggling to catch up to him.

"Wow. I just kind of assumed that having magic would make it easier for your enforcers to catch criminals and put them behind bars," Natalie mused as Alia pulled up yet another case file. This one looked the most recent, although it was also a bit vague and had been almost hidden in the stack of other files.

Alia read through, and her jaw dropped open. "Looks like he really pissed off the enforcers this time. "His latest crime and the one that they are really trying to hunt him down for is against the enforcer division here in the city themselves."

Natalie's forehead creased in confusion. "He conned the enforcers?"

"Apparently, he charmed his way into an enforcer's office and destroyed or stole a bunch of evidence in other werewolf cases."

"Wow. That's…like, he helped a bunch of his own kind get away with crimes despite being a lone wolf."

"Yeah. It doesn't entirely make sense, but some of the werewolf packs are very powerful and have a lot of money. It's possible that they paid him a lot of money to get them off from some kind of crime. Especially if they were young werewolves."

Natalie exhaled as Alia read and Rich gave Lucas head scritches. This was fascinating stuff. It wasn't one or two packs that Francisco had helped. The enforcer report read like it was tons of them. As if it was possibly every active werewolf case.

Alia told the others what she was reading, and they listened with wide eyes.

"No wonder they wanted it all hushed up and don't want to give too many details," Natalie mused. "They're ashamed of this. Of what he achieved."

"I would be too. Might mean a *really* big reward though." Rich looked apologetically at Lucas as he spoke.

"We need money as well," Lucas agreed, present enough still to at least pick up on that.

"We're not going to give up on you." Natalie reached over and stroked him.

"I know. And I can help too. But let's do what we can to earn while we go and not ruin ourselves along the way. I need you all to keep buying me the good food. I want tuna fish steaks every day I'm a proper cat."

"We are definitely going to get you good food. Don't worry about that. But we also intend to get you back to your human self in no time at all. We've just got to find the right piece of missing information."

CHAPTER FOUR

"All right." Rich focused on the case the others were looking into. The AR glasses were working again and he was out of leads for curing Lucas.

That left one task for them to focus on: finding this Francisco werewolf and bringing him to justice.

"So, where are we going to start?" he asked.

"Where do you want to?" Alia replied. She continued clicking through the records on the man.

Rich sat on the opposite side of her from Natalie. At first, he simply read over Alia's shoulder and tried to take everything in and understand it. It used a lot of jargon, which made it harder to work out what they were trying to say.

Alia read faster than Rich and Natalie, and she gasped.

"What?" they replied in unison.

"It says here that Francisco was last seen in France at a villa he has there." Alia looked impressed as she pulled up photos of the residence. The place was huge.

"France? Does that mean we are being asked to follow

him there? If we need to do so they better be paying and making sure that our glasses can get there along with us and not get lost in baggage claim or other possibilities right away," Natalie said.

Rich shrugged. "I guess we're going to France at some point."

"Now?" Natalie asked.

"We might have to if we do actually want to take this case on." Alia looked through the notes some more. "It sounds like he might not be there for very long."

Natalie bit her lip again then sighed.

"Okay. I haven't traveled for a while. If we can persuade the police department to pay for our flights and somewhere to stay at the other end, then I guess we could go."

"Do you all have passports?" Alia asked.

"We all do, but I might need to remind you that I don't look anything like my picture currently." Lucas wore the disdainful expression that most cats wore whether they were unimpressed or not.

"We'll have to see what cats require to travel." Natalie went back to her computer and started typing.

Lucas didn't look any happier. "I'm not going to sit in some quarantine for weeks while you all have an adventure."

"It's okay, you shouldn't have to as long as we can meet all the requirements for entry," Natalie called over her shoulder as she continued to type and research.

Rich felt useless. Both Alia and Natalie were busy doing something to help while he sat there with some temporarily fixed glasses in his hand.

"Okay, looks like we need to have a set of rabies shots

signed off by a vet to avoid quarantine," Natalie reported a few seconds later.

"I'm not letting you hit me with a bunch of shots for something I'm not actually going to get." Lucas padded across the desks toward Natalie.

"And a microchip." She winced. "None of this is going to really work."

"I might be able to help," Rich replied. "There's a vet in my hometown. A guy I used to play with when we were kids. I saved his ass one time and now he owes me. I might be able to get him to help us. It means telling someone else about magic though."

Alia looked doubtful. "I don't think that's a good idea."

"Do we have a choice, if we want to go to France and we want to take Lucas with us?" Natalie swiveled around in her seat so she was facing everyone again.

"Not sure you guys are listening properly," Lucas interrupted. "I don't want to have any of this stuff done to me. And I know that you won't make me do anything I don't want to do. Not even in cat form."

"You don't want to do *any* of this. We could leave you here. Book you into one of those cat kennel places. Somewhere you can enjoy the cat food, head scritches, and fighting over things like mice and rats." Natalie smiled, and for a second she looked as if she might enjoy such a threat.

"There's no way you're putting me in some kind of cat home. What if they decide that they're going to be one of those dodgy ones? I could end up being sold to a Chinese restaurant or something."

Lucas had a point, but it amused Rich that the guy was so afraid of everything right now that even going to a kennel was scary and terrifying and he assumed the worst. He reminded himself that it was shitty of him to enjoy his friend's discomfort.

"It's cat home or we work out a way to trick a vet or persuade a vet to help us get you a special medical license." Rich felt sorry for Lucas, but he was making life harder on himself. The easiest thing for him to do was let things happen as they happened.

It was important for all of them to be able to help him if he didn't want it any harder on them. Not that Rich blamed him for not wanting to be microchipped or get a vaccine for something unnecessary.

"I really do know a guy," Rich insisted a moment later.

"I don't doubt it," Alia shot back. "It's you telling him about magic that isn't wise. The enforcers will jump at every reason to wipe your memories. Or worse. There will be no saving Lucas if you all have that happen to you."

"You wouldn't try and save me if they couldn't?" The cat rolled onto his side and looked up at Alia imploringly.

"As much as I'd want to try, the enforcers would forbid me from ever seeing any of you again. I'd be lucky to spend the next few years in prison and that would just be for attempting to talk to you three again in some way. Actually trying to turn Lucas back into a human? I'd be in big trouble for that. It's bad enough that I talked to you at all."

"I think, given Lucas is stuck as a cat and could need a vet for other reasons before we get him back to being human, that this is a risk we should take." Rich leaned forward and stuck out his chin, almost daring the other three of them to challenge him or tell him that he was wrong.

"How well do you know him?" Natalie asked.

"I haven't talked to him in a few years, but he was a good guy. If he can wrap his head around magic then he'd have our back. If nothing else he's likely to appreciate us making his life more interesting."

That seemed to settle it. The others nodded and Rich reached for his phone.

"Don't tell him anything over the phone," Alia suggested.

It was a good point. If the enforcers were keeping an eye on them, it made sense to be careful.

"Okay, Natalie, go sort out the travel arrangements with Alia. Me and Lucas will go see a vet about some stuff and we'll go from there."

Within seconds, everyone was on their feet. Rich was shocked for a moment. They'd been sitting around researching for days to cure Lucas and now they were off on another whirlwind adventure.

As Natalie got to the door, she held out her hand as if to take the glasses from Rich, but he and Alia said no at the same time.

"They're the easiest thing to use to persuade that vet that it's all true," Alia explained.

"Hey, I'm not agreeing to this," Lucas protested. "I do not want to go to a vet, even one Rich knows, to be prodded and poked by some guy I've never met and be jabbed and chipped and God knows what else. It just isn't happening."

"Come on, Lucas." Rich was already frustrated. They'd just come up with a possible solution and now he was deciding to be awkward about it.

"Nope." Before any of them could stop him, Lucas darted out of the open door and ran off.

Natalie swore and Alia growled. It was not turning into a good day.

"Change of plans, I guess." Rich handed the glasses over to Natalie after all. "I guess you might as well learn what you can about this Francisco guy while I wait for Lucas and think of some way to drug him or something."

"I can get something to put him out cold," Alia offered. "Put it in his food."

It was about the best plan they could come up with, all things considered. If Lucas didn't come back soon, he would when he was hungry and they would have to make sure he did what they needed. With any luck, it would be quick and painless, and Rich's friend would help them without having to do anything to the unfortunate cat.

CHAPTER FIVE

Natalie liked wearing the glasses and being able to see all the information that they provided, but there were times when it could also be overwhelming. Given where Alia had brought them, this was one of the latter situations.

A couple of times, she had gone to remove the glasses and give herself a break, but each time Alia had stopped her. When she went to do it for a third time, beginning to get a headache, Alia stopped and rounded on her.

"You really need to keep those on," she half-whispered and half-threatened.

"Why?" Natalie asked, but she lowered her hand.

"Because we're in an area with a lot of magical folk, and you want to know that danger is coming before it arrives. I know what warning signs to pick up on and there's a chance those glasses do too, but you don't. I don't want your death on my hands today. Not to mention all the other possibilities of consequences if you piss off the wrong person while in here."

Natalie nodded, gulping as she did. When Alia had said

something about getting a sedative for Lucas and more information on Francisco at the same time, she had envisioned something much more like popping into a shop and asking for it. Instead, they were wandering around what appeared to be the magical equivalent of a flea market.

Everywhere Natalie looked, the glasses were feeding her information on fantastical races and people with magical abilities. Most had both, but some were only one or the other. And there were a lot of people.

"We need to find a friend I know who can get ahold of the sedative we need," Alia explained.

"Okay, what or who am I looking for?" Natalie continued to scan and hoped she didn't appear to be staring at anyone.

"He's a short guy, barely up to your chest. Got a bit of a swagger. Half-gnome and half-elf... Don't ask."

"Name?" Natalie switched her attention to anyone she could look over. There weren't many people that fit that bill, even with the huge number of fantastical people in front of her.

It was strange to see all the items as well. The glasses occasionally filled in information on what some of the teapots, umbrellas, and other bric-a-brac could do on top of their original purpose.

Natalie couldn't take it all in, but now that she had something to look for, it wasn't so overwhelming. Her mind was able to disregard the huge amounts of text popping up over her view.

They rambled through the market, and Alia stuck close to Natalie to help guide her. It was necessary, as they were jostled several times and a few people glared at Natalie when she bumped into them.

"Careful," Alia hissed and pulled Natalie out of the way of a particularly mean-looking warlock.

Aware that this might have been one of the dangers Alia had been talking about earlier, Natalie tensed up. She didn't want to get turned into a frog or anything else. Or worse.

"I think I see him," Natalie murmured a few seconds later when a gnome flashed up on her screen.

As she read the whole set of text, she realized she was wrong. She'd found a large stall with *several* gnomes staffing it. They were selling a home brew. Some of it listed magical properties, like making a person taller, or growing hair and beards.

Everything around Natalie was fascinating, if only she'd had the time for it.

"Close," Alia whispered. "But not who we're looking for. He is a bit of a gnome outcast, but he's not likely to be too far away."

They walked for another half hour before Natalie spotted him and pointed him out.

He was standing behind a much smaller stall, this one covered in what looked like hunting equipment. There were rifles, tranquilizer darts, nets, and all sorts of other equipment that also came with magical enchantments. The nets came with some kind of lightning buff. Natalie assumed this made it an electrified net of some kind but didn't dare ask.

"Graham!" Alia beamed as they approached the stall and the half-gnome looked over at them.

"Alia. Long time no see. How's my favorite elf?"

"I'm the *only* elf who will talk to you." She raised her hand to fist-bump him.

"That might be true, but you'd still be my favorite even if the others did acknowledge that I exist. What can I help you with? You look like you're on a mission. And with an amagical human in tow? Don't you remember the rules?"

"She's cool. Allowed. Helping me, even. She's got a few gifts that the average magic user doesn't, but we have a bit of a problem. Got a cat that isn't a cat to take on holiday with us and the only thing we can think of doing is to tranquilize the poor guy."

The gnome frowned and looked at his wares for a moment before pulling out several options.

"Okay, I'm going to need more information to narrow it down. What do you mean by 'is a cat but isn't a cat'? Some kind of shifter, like a werewolf?" He picked up the first dose of tranquilizer that would fit into one of his guns and lifted it up. "'Cause this would work on a normal cat, but nothing bigger than normal."

"He was cursed. Daven Hoth."

"The guy who died in that explosion last week?" Graham asked, eyebrows raised.

"Yeah… And I know. Curses are meant to break when the person who cast them dies. We're getting a little sick of hearing that when somehow it's not what happened."

"That's rough. And you want to knock this guy out for a bit?"

Alia nodded and spent the next fifteen minutes explaining everything to Graham. While she did, Natalie took the opportunity to look around a bit more. The next stall was selling an array of different-sized glass bottles, each with its own contents ranging from large liter bottles of fuchsia liquids to tiny bottles with nothing in them but a drop of something black and slimy looking.

The glasses fed her information on most of them, although a few of the potions had a row of question marks in the name and description. It wasn't the first time the glasses hadn't been able to identify something, but it made Natalie more curious and she wanted to go over and ask about the bottles.

She was most fascinated that some were labeled love potions and others seemed to flaunt being hallucinogenic. It struck her as a strange thing when the world was so anti-drugs, and these didn't look to be very expensive.

"Right, we'd best have several. Just in case." Alia tapped on Natalie's arm to get her attention.

She turned back to her companion to see Graham lift a case of six tranquilizer darts and the gun that fired them.

"If the gun isn't your preferred method of delivery and said cat is at least a little cooperative, you can also put these into an applicator that you can use with your hand. That's a little cheaper, but if he's a little awkward as a friend, the gun might be satisfying."

Alia and Natalie laughed. It might be a little wrong, but Natalie was sure that she'd enjoy it. Alia stashed the new item away safely.

As they moved on, Natalie drew Alia's attention to the stall close by.

"Do things like love potions actually work?" she asked.

"Why? Got someone in mind to use it on?" Alia grinned and winked.

Natalie laughed but shook her head. Although Rich clearly had a crush on Alia, she was not going to get one for him to use, and Natalie didn't mind being single. She had no intention of using one.

"I honestly don't know," Alia admitted. "I've heard people swear by them, and others say they're nothing but bullshit. Like anything else magical, it probably depends on the person creating it. Some of the best magicians I know, I wouldn't put it past them."

"Not sure if that's awesome or not." Natalie bit her lip and Alia led her onward.

"I know. The same magicians also all warned me that messing with free will like that often comes with a price. You don't get to screw around with people's hearts and not risk your own or something."

"That's more than enough to put me off ever trying one." Natalie shuddered, but she glanced over the stall one last time anyway, wondering if the others could ever be useful. If anything, so far she'd already learned that magic wasn't as fun as the stories made out when she was younger. It was complicated and messy, and it could go wrong. That was all she needed to know to pay it plenty of respect.

Alia kept them going instead of going back, and she stopped at a few stalls to catch up with old friends. At each of them, she introduced Natalie and brought up their need to break the cat curse followed by mentions of Francisco. None of it yielded anything, but Natalie appreciated the young elf's efforts.

By the time Natalie's feet ached and her eyes hurt from looking through the glasses for so long, she was ready to head back to the car and get on with their mission. Alia had other plans, however.

"I need you to stay right here. Don't talk to anyone. Don't stare at anyone. And if someone gets aggressive with you, head in that direction and keep going until you get to a stall covered in pies. There will be a woman there and if you tell her you're a friend of Alia's and she sent you to get dinner, I should be able to get to you before anyone will bother you further."

Natalie opened her mouth to ask questions and object to the plan, but Alia had already moved away and pulled back the flap on a large tent.

For the next few minutes, Natalie did her best to look as if she were browsing and minding her own business. Now that Alia had stressed not to stare at people for the second time, she felt more conscious about looking anywhere too long.

The woman at the nearest stall asked Natalie if she could help. It was a stall of old books and Natalie was browsing through the titles, wondering what sort of thing the magical world wanted to read about.

"You might be able to, actually. My friend has been cursed and turned into a cat." Natalie explained the predicament without naming any names or giving too many details away. After getting past the initial, "if the caster was dead the curse should be broken" problem everyone was having, the woman tilted her head to the side.

"That's quite a problem, and make no mistake. I've not got a book here that I think can help right now, but I know a few folks. I can ask around. If you've not solved the problem in a few weeks, come back to me and I'll try and have a direction I can point you in. In the meantime, I notice that rosy complexion of yours could do with a little boost."

As the woman continued to waffle on about Natalie's looks, complimenting and insulting her all at the same time, she picked up an old book about natural remedies for physical issues and tried to sell it to Natalie.

"Oh, I've got a copy of that I can lend you," Alia offered as she reappeared at Natalie's side.

The woman scowled and put it back down again, and Alia took Natalie's arm to lead her away.

"Can never be too careful buying anything in here," Alia added before smiling. "Right, shall we go find the guys and get Lucas to the vet?"

CHAPTER SIX

Rich frowned as he shut the door and Lucas sat on the sofa.

"I'm not doing it," Lucas insisted. "I'm not going to a vet so he can jab me and stick a chip in me."

"What choice do we have?" Rich took a step closer, but Lucas jumped back and moved toward the stairs.

Rich had confirmed every window and door was shut, but he didn't doubt that Lucas could get out of the house again. The man might be in cat form, but he had enough intelligence left to be able to open windows and possibly even pull on door handles. Being a cat didn't make him stupid. It just took away his opposable thumbs.

In the back of his mind, he wondered where Natalie and Alia had gotten off to. They were taking ages finding something to help. Not that it would make it any easier to get it into Lucas. The cat wasn't going to let them knock him out.

"There's got to be another way. I'm a person, not a cat. Maybe if I just talked to the right person, I could—"

"We both know that we have to be careful who we talk to."

"But it's okay to talk to the vet you know?"

"I'm not sure it is." Rich sat, exhausted already by this whole fiasco and also wanting to appear as nonthreatening as possible.

It made Lucas relax and for a few minutes, the two of them chatted about regular friend things.

Before long, Lucas's ears pricked up, and he turned toward the front door. A few seconds later, Rich also heard the sound of the car returning. Alia and Natalie were back, and he hoped they had something to help.

If nothing else, it would give them something to do. He didn't want to admit it to his best friend, but they didn't have a clue how to get him back out of cat form.

Rich got up and went to the door, hoping to be able to talk to Alia and Natalie before they came back into the house and Lucas heard, but the cat followed him at a distance.

When he got outside, he saw Alia and Natalie still inside the car. Natalie put her finger to her lips as Alia raised a pistol and held up what looked like a strange dart.

While he watched Lucas in the house behind him, she loaded the weapon with a couple of tranquilizers.

It was a solution that Rich hadn't thought of, but he saw the appeal in it. He wasn't a good shot, but he had a feeling he wasn't going to need to be. Alia had a strange glint in her eyes as she got out of the car and chucked him the keys.

"In there," Rich mouthed and stepped aside so she could get through.

"Please don't tell me that you want me to chow down

on some disgusting pills of some kind either," Lucas began when he spotted Alia. "No, no, no…"

She chuckled, and Rich followed her inside in time to see Lucas spot the pistol and run for the back door in the kitchen. Alia strode after him with the pistol raised.

As the cat reached the door and tried to jump up to get the handle, she fired. The dart hit him in the middle of the back, not far from his shoulder blades.

"Ouch!" he yelled as he hit the ground. "You're despicable friends…"

The sedative kicked in almost immediately, and he flopped over. Alia pumped her fist in the air.

"Still got it," she declared with the biggest grin Rich had ever seen on her face.

"Wow. I had no idea you could shoot," Rich remarked as Natalie handed him a pet carrier they'd bought while they were out.

Gently, the three of them eased the poor sleeping Lucas into the carrier and added in a cat toy to make it seem as if this was a real cat to an outside observer.

"We should get this over with," Natalie added, looking as if she might cry.

He couldn't blame her. Doing this to Lucas felt wrong. But they were trying to save him and avoid getting their memories wiped.

"I'll take him to the vet and chat with my friend." Rich picked up the carrier.

"Don't tell the vet if you don't have to that Lucas is actually a person. Just get him to approve the travel for the cat and reassure him that we'll keep it away from any others." Alia looked him in the eye, standing in his way for a moment.

Rich frowned. Although he knew it was wise, he didn't like lying. To the vet *or* to Lucas. They'd implied to Lucas that they wouldn't vaccinate him if not necessary, and Rich didn't feel comfortable doing that. But the enforcers were looking for any reason to wipe their memories, and if that happened Lucas would forever be stuck as a cat.

Rather than say that, he replied, "We should get everything else we need to travel and make sure all our stuff here is going to be safe for a few days."

"Got it, boss," Natalie replied with a grin.

"I know someone who can watch our stuff for us. We'll be cooperating with the enforcers over in France so it's not like they're going to kick us out of here or confiscate anything while we're gone. They can be shitty, but they're never that shitty." Alia tucked the pistol back in its case along with the remaining darts.

As soon as Rich had the cat carrier in the car, he drove off.

The vet was fairly busy, but it also progressed swiftly and the office left space for emergency appointments. He talked to the receptionist and made up a reason to need to see the vet ASAP, then waited his turn.

Thankfully, his friend let him in quickly.

"Rich! What are you doing here? Didn't know you were in the area again." Jim helped him get the carrier onto the table.

"I need your help," Rich replied, hoping he wasn't about to get chucked out.

"Sick pets are what I can help with."

"He's not as sick as I told the lovely lady you've got on reception out there, and I'm sorry for lying to get to see you. I've just got myself in a bit of a mess and I can't see any harm come to my cat because of it."

"Well, I must admit that I wouldn't normally have pity on anyone telling me something like that. Why don't you start this story from the beginning, and I'll see what I can do, but you'd better hurry, I'm not going to give you long. I have a lot of pets out there that need my help."

Rich apologized again and then launched into the fake story he'd concocted on the way there. It wasn't ideal, but it was the best he'd been able to come up with on short notice. He told Jim about having to go to France for a work-related thing and having no choice financially and having to take the cat because the cat was part of the project he needed the money for.

It was a strange story and he saw Jim frown more than a few times.

"And you definitely need the cat with you?"

"Yes. If I don't take the cat this isn't going to work at all. And I can't afford not to go. I'm living with a friend as it is and they're almost out of money too. We're both on the streets if this doesn't work." The last part was at least true, and it seemed to sway his friend.

"Okay, I can give him at least one of the rabies shots and get him microchipped and I can sign off the paperwork to say he's safe to travel, but I warn you, that if this ever gets out I will throw you under the bus."

"I will never tell a soul. If you don't tell anyone ever either then it's never going to be discovered. I swear." Rich looked as sincere as he could. Technically, there were three other people who already knew, including the cat himself, but he doubted any of them were going to risk any more trouble and ever talk about it either.

"Leave him with me and pick him up tomorrow morning. I'll need time to sort this out."

"Thank you so much." Rich shook Jim's hand. "I'll make sure to pay your bills as if we did the whole lot you'd need to in the right order."

"You'd better, and I'm going to charge you for three vet visits to do it all as well."

"Understood."

As he walked away and out of the vet's he exhaled with relief. Then he thought of Lucas coming around while at the vet's and not knowing where he was. With all the will in the world, they couldn't have kept their secret safe. It made him feel guilty, however. This wasn't what he'd have hoped for, for any of them.

It made him wonder if they should walk away from the magical world altogether, but they were on thin ice with the enforcers and they had to get Lucas back in human form. For now, they would keep the enforcers happy and keep trying to find a cure. He hoped they didn't get themselves killed or into too much trouble in the meantime.

CHAPTER SEVEN

As Alia picked out a suitcase alongside Natalie she felt a thrill of delight. With everything she'd faced and all the difficulties she'd had just getting by in life, she'd never left the country, and now she was going to get to. On official enforcer business no less. Knowing that it was all being paid for by the enforcers was a strange feeling.

Natalie's grin was as wide as Alia's and she was just as excited when she picked out her own luggage and everything she needed to go with it.

"Do you think we should get some new clothes as well?" Natalie asked. "I have no idea what the weather is like in France at this time of year."

"I definitely think new clothes are a good idea. I don't know about you, but I don't have a lot, and if this investigation takes a while and we're trying to catch this guy we need plenty of options and won't want to be doing a bunch of laundry." Alia spoke as calmly as she could, as if it was the most obvious response, unsure how Natalie would take the implied desire to buy lots of clothes.

"Very good point. We should make sure that Rich does the same. Want to help me pick him out a few things as well?"

Alia nodded. This was a day in heaven as far as she was concerned. Although she'd had doubts about working with these three, and the first time she'd met Rich she had thought he was a clueless moron who had stumbled upon something that could get him in a lot of trouble, she had to admit that they were a solid set of folks.

The enforcers had never treated her with as much respect as they had earlier that day. They'd still been heavy-handed and bordered on threatening, but they'd talked to her as if they needed her as well as Natalie and Rich. And Natalie, Lucas, and Rich were all treating her as if she was part of their group now. It felt good.

Over the course of the next two hours, they shopped. Rich joined them near the end but did nothing other than express his gratitude that they'd thought to get some of what he needed. With Lucas taken care of, they were at liberty to do as they pleased for the rest of the day as well, and they even had dinner out.

By the time the day was over and their tickets were booked to fly with a cat the following day, Alia was exhausted but excited. She didn't let any of it stop her, though.

Once the three of them got back to Alia's pad in the Unplace, they all sat at their computers. Natalie went back to her work to keep the business with the glasses ticking along while Rich looked for ways to turn Lucas back into a human. That left more research on Francisco for Alia.

She'd grabbed all the information the enforcers had in

the system and she went through it again, trying to work out if there were any patterns to this guy's behavior or any way he might try to trap them.

There wasn't a lot to go on, but she liked to be prepared for a mission when she could. And this was a mission, if different from the usual thieveries and scams she planned. She would be on the other side of the law for starters, but there were some similarities. They had to figure this guy out and she was excited about it.

The group worked long into the night, breaking to sleep before Rich got a call to go pick Lucas up. With everything else ready, they all opted to go get him together. Partially because Alia didn't want to miss how angry he was going to be. She took the pistol and darts with her, just in case.

If nothing else, she wanted Lucas to know it was there if he was a major pain in the ass on the return journey. It was a bit mean of her maybe, but she wouldn't use it on him unless he made it impossible otherwise.

It took a couple of hours to get to the vet, but it was a nice drive and the furthest Alia had been in years. She enjoyed seeing how amagicals lived along the way. It looked a little boring, but it also looked as if it might be simpler.

The vet brought Lucas out to them in the cat carrier not long after they arrived.

"I'll send you my bill before the end of the day, as discussed," the vet let him know.

"And he's okay?" Rich asked.

"Yes. He's out cold again. We were worried about him. Started making the strangest meows while he was woozy and coming around. Almost sounded like words. I didn't want him to be distressed so we sedated him again."

"Thank you, Jim. I really appreciate it. I won't forget your help."

"See you don't forget what we talked about." The vet looked at everyone in the car as he finished speaking, and Alia wondered what he could be worried about. Had Rich told him something, even when they'd decided it was best not to?

As Rich handed the carrier to Natalie, Lucas stirred and mumbled in his sleep. Something unintelligible, but it made Alia frown. It had been a close call if Lucas had been talking in his sleep. Not ideal.

"He really seems out of it. Do you think he's okay?" Natalie asked.

"Might not be right now, but we'll get him back and get him something he loves to eat and hope he forgives us."

"I miss having him in human form." Natalie's eyes watered up, but she held the emotion back and Alia felt a pang in her heart in response. These three really cared about each other.

"We'll break the curse," Alia promised. "We're doing everything we can."

Natalie gave her a grateful nod, and Alia returned the gesture. It was time to get their last affairs in order, pack and go get on a plane. They were booked on a red-eye flight to hop across to Europe, and that gave them a few hours still to pack, get Lucas sorted, and get to the airport.

Although she hadn't said anything to the others, Alia was also nervous about her passport. She hadn't told them she didn't have one. She had paid an acquaintance in the marketplace to get her one when she'd been there the day before, but he might flake on her.

She worried about it all the ride back as Lucas woke up more and started to shuffle around the carrier. He talked to them about nonsense a couple of times.

"Alia, you rat. I knew you were a thief. I didn't think you were also the son of a motherless goat," Lucas slurred out a bit later.

Natalie stifled a giggle as he fell over and back asleep again.

"It's really tempting to record this and play it back to him later," Rich added a moment later. "Something we can bring up if he ever complains about us being drunk again."

"The temptation is real," Natalie agreed with a light flashing in her eyes, but neither of them did it.

The silly antics of the slowly waking cat kept them amused during the journey back to the Unplace, and Alia helped carry him inside as he stirred again.

"Home… Ow. What did you all do to my ass? It feels like someone stuffed one butt cheek with cotton wool or something. It's all pressured and ouch."

"Side effect of the medication, I'm afraid." Natalie went to open the carrier, but before she could, Rich stopped her.

"We need him in there to take him on the plane. Best to leave him for now. There's no way he's going to willingly go back inside."

"What about if he needs to go to the bathroom?" she asked.

Rich frowned for a moment and then took the carrier and headed to the nearest restroom. Grinning in amusement, Alia watched him go. Her enjoyment of the situation only lasted a moment, however, and the worry about her passport set in again.

They packed and Rich came back, Lucas still in and out and hurling crazy sentences, rarely coherent over the next hour.

Natalie was sitting on Alia's suitcase so it would close when someone knocked at the door. It wasn't the normal knock, but a couple of quick taps, several longer ones, and then a pattern of harder and softer ones.

The elf went to the door and pulled it open enough that she could see outside but blocked the opening with her body so no one else could see out.

"It took a little more effort than usual at short notice, so you owe me, Alia, but here it is." The gnome on the other side of the door looked around as if he expected to be arrested or seen by someone at any moment.

"Thank you. I'll pay you back in kind as soon as I'm back."

"You better come back."

"I always do, don't I?" she replied.

"Aye. If nothing else, I know you're good for your word when you give it. At least to the likes of us. But you better be careful. Some say that you've gone enforcer side. That they've got something on you and you're giving them info."

"No. As I said, I've got a cursed friend and I am doing the bare minimum I need to get them to help break it. You know I won't break the code."

The gnome studied her for a moment then nodded.

"All right. See you on the other side."

"On the other side," she repeated. It was a phrase she'd said many times, and it didn't feel wrong to say it now. She was going to France to catch a criminal she didn't entirely disagree with, but she was still on a mission of sorts. And it wasn't necessarily breaking the code.

She'd seen some of the evidence Francisco had stolen from the French enforcers. It was stuff that would have incriminated genuine criminals. The kind of werewolves who had done things like Daven had and hurt people.

The criminals she associated with and that she'd stolen for had a code. You didn't take anything from anyone who genuinely needed it. No taking food from a poor family. No taking the magical item someone needed for their livelihood. No screwing over the little guy. It wasn't a perfect system, but it meant she targeted people who could afford to lose what she was taking.

It was a Robin Hood approach to thievery, and the people who were willing to commit crimes along with her were those sorts of people.

As she turned to face the room behind her, she noticed the looks on Natalie and Rich's faces. They had questions.

"Is that a forged passport?" Rich asked, hitting the nail straight on the head. Seeing no point in denying it, Alia nodded.

"Is it going to be okay?" Natalie added, concern, not judgment, was written on her features. "Are you going to get in trouble trying to use that just to help us?"

"Not if my guy is as good as he says he is," Alia assured them after a moment of thought.

This made them both relax.

"You could have told us about it, you know," Rich told her. "We might not have done some of the things you have, but we get it."

"Noted." Alia relaxed for the first time in ages.

"I don't care either," Lucas called from the carrier now sitting by the kitchen table. "Not that you asked. Just no shooting me again. Or making me go somewhere I don't want to go. And for that matter, let me out of this stupid box."

Shuffling around, Lucas tried to paw at all sorts of angles, lucid for a moment before he started spouting nonsense again.

"Should we put him out of his misery and keep him from saying something he shouldn't during the flight?" Natalie asked.

"No, no more. I want to feel the wind in my hair. I want to be in the clouds. To sit on the wings and see the world go by. The tiny oceans and the even tinier whales."

Rich put a hand over his mouth to hide his grin as he pointed to the pouch where Alia had kept the pistol. Not needing either of them to suggest it again, she got it out and loaded another shot. By the time she had it ready, Lucas was already waffling on about flying on the wings of eagles and some random conversation he'd apparently had the night before with a bird.

Within another couple of seconds, she had put him out of his misery again and there was once more silence.

"Finally, maybe we can think. Let's gather the last few things we need and head to the airport." Rich moved the carrier to the front door and started piling up the suitcases beside it.

Feeling a mix of excitement and apprehension, Alia slung the pistol to one side and pulled her boots on again. It was time to visit a whole new part of the world.

CHAPTER EIGHT

The ride to the airport flew by in a haze of anticipation for Natalie. It had been a few years since she'd flown, but she remembered the flights all too well. While she'd been growing up, they had been a regular thing. She remembered the stress in the house as her parents packed for ski trips, or summer vacations and long breaks.

Although she hadn't said anything to the others, she had been to Europe several times. She had different memories of arguments, strange places her parents had dragged her in the name of business for her father or spiritual enlightenment for her mother. She didn't have a problem with either, but she'd wanted to go to museums, to castles, and to interesting bookshops.

Maybe this time, with her friends it would be different. At least, she hoped it would be. She wanted to enjoy the trip, and it helped that Alia appeared to be excited.

"There's a bunch of less fun stuff to do first," Rich reminded them as they pulled the luggage from the car trunk and he picked up the cat carrier again. Lucas was out cold and snoring gently in a catlike fashion.

"Yeah, checking in, making sure our baggage isn't too heavy, and then security."

"That why you told me to put the knives in my suitcase and not in my boots?" Alia replied.

Natalie heard a hint of both sadness and annoyance in the young elf's voice at this statement, but she nodded.

"What comes after security?"

"If nothing goes wrong and both of those are relatively light on traffic, a long wait in front of what's called a gate. It's not much of a gate though. More like a door to a tunnel or an exit onto the runway. We'll get called onto the plane in groups. We've got relatively good seats but not the best, so we're likely to be called up somewhere in the middle."

"Sounds like fun. I've never been more important than the cheapest tickets for anything before." Alia grinned. "What perks do we get?"

"In premium economy, mostly slightly bigger seats and better headphones." Rich shifted the carrier.

His words made Alia beam and reminded Natalie that her childhood had been very different. She'd never flown in anything less than business, and in her own way, she was as clueless as Alia was.

Without any more delay, they hurried into the airport to check in their bags. Lucas counted as a carry-on for one of them and they had managed to get all their suitcases under the weight allowance.

Alia clutched her boarding pass, studying it and all the information on it and holding the passport that went with it. She'd grown tense when she had to hand over the forgery, but the guy on the desk had barely looked at it or the group, having already checked Natalie's and no longer being concerned in any way.

Although the others had told her not to carry her usual array of daggers and tools through security and to put them in her suitcase instead, she didn't know what to expect from this. Natalie walked her through it while Rich focused on getting Lucas through security.

It felt strange to her to put all her belongings in a box, empty all her pockets, and put anything electronic on show. The weirdest part was taking off her boots and walking through the strange booth with her hands in the air.

She studied Natalie doing everything, letting the young woman lead her through what to do. She felt tense until she was through the other side and putting her boots back on, though.

There weren't any problems. The woman checking the boxes as they went through the X-ray machine was distracted by the cat. Even with Lucas out cold, everyone wanted to make a fuss over him.

Alia wondered if it would always be best to take through lots of personal items when doing something dodgy at an airport. If you looked like a tourist, everyone assumed you were harmless. If you looked like you loved animals, you were thought even more highly of.

The interplay of social dynamics had always fascinated Alia and she didn't deny that she'd used it to her advantage on more than one occasion. She could never stop thinking of the angles and the potential for thievery or a con of some kind. Everything was a trick or a deception in her mind.

She was tired of it. Tired of always being suspicious. Tired of thinking she could be caught at any moment. It was going to feel different trying to catch a criminal this time.

She hoped people would understand. This wasn't something she was doing for the enforcers.

Once they had everything gathered and were on the other side, Natalie checked the time and declared that they still had two hours and could shop and eat. This part Alia hadn't expected. She didn't have to go far before she was overwhelmed by the shops and restaurants crammed into such a small space.

Natalie grabbed her arm and whisked her off to look at perfume and jewelry, and Alia marveled at how easy it would have been to steal a phenomenal amount of goods and make the cost of the ticket back easily.

None of it came close to her excitement about getting to go on a plane, however. When they arrived at the gate, they were early enough to see the plane come up to park and be prepared for takeoff.

She went over to the glass to look at the plane closer, marveling at how something so large could fly so seemingly effortlessly through the sky. It was strange to her eyes, but it was a new experience and she'd always wanted to travel.

Lucas remained out of it as they were called to go to their seats. As Rich had said, they weren't in the first batch of passengers to board, but they were in the third group.

Natalie led the way again as they hurried to go to their seats.

Alia stared at everything, fascinated. There were such strange seats in the first area, laid-back pods where people could have their own private experience, followed by slightly less closed-off areas and large seats that still looked quite comfortable.

Natalie pointed to a row of black leather seats, each one more than large enough for the three of them, although with Rich having to have Lucas in his carrier, a lot of the room on their row was taken up by that. They stowed almost everything else above them and settled into their seats.

For the first few minutes, Alia was distracted by the blanket, pillow, and headphones each seat had on them. It was like being given a gift, but she guessed she was just borrowing it. She got even more excited when Natalie showed her how to work the entertainment screen and they flipped through all sorts of movie options.

The flight wasn't full, and that gave them a little more room to spread out, but it was full enough that staff and people continued to bustle past them for several minutes.

When they were ready to take off, Natalie pointed to the small windows on the side of the plane as they sped along the runway. The plane jolted and bumped, but less than Alia feared it would, and then they were suddenly smoothly gliding, and a feeling of weightlessness came over her.

Her eyes went wide as she gripped the sides of her seat. Seeing her reaction, Natalie chuckled.

"You'll get used to it in a moment."

Alia's brain felt a little fuzzy. She opened her mouth to tell Natalie she felt weird, but her words came out in the wrong order.

Rich laughed, a sound that seemed extra shrill and loud. She flinched and almost bumped into Natalie.

"Seems like elves don't react well to flying." Natalie waved her hand in front of Alia's face before she reached into her small bag and pulled out some wrapped hard candy. "Here, try this. It might help the pressure equalize in you more quickly."

Knowing something wasn't right with how she felt, Alia grabbed the offered sweet and shoved it in her mouth. In a few minutes, she felt a little better, but her mind still felt strange no matter what she did, and she had trouble focusing.

"Would you like the chicken or the vegetarian?" the steward asked when he came past their seats pulling a trolley.

"Both?" Alia replied. "What am I choosing? Are we going to let some animals loose? Good thing the cat is out cold."

"She'll have the chicken." Natalie frowned at her for a moment.

"What?" Alia didn't know what her problem was.

"He's asking what you want for dinner," Rich explained in a whisper as Natalie took a tray of food for her and put it down in front of her.

Understanding dawned on her and she looked up and gave the steward a big thumbs-up and grinned.

He raised his eyebrows, but then Natalie was asking for her and Rich's meals.

"I think we need to have you not talk to the people and you should sleep or something," Natalie suggested gently, opening Alia's blanket and pillow package.

Although she wanted to protest, it seemed like too much trouble. She felt funny and light-headed. Food and then a nap might do her some good.

After all, they did give her a blanket and a pillow.

CHAPTER NINE

Amazed by his luck, Rich exited the apartment the enforcers had rented for them in Paris with Alia. Natalie had decided she needed to do some more work and put together a press release that didn't say anything but would keep people happy.

On top of that, she was going to watch Lucas, who was still pretty much out of it. The combined effect of so many tranquilizers and sedatives was that he was still snoring away in cat form.

All this meant that Rich had the company of a woman he had a crush on, and he was in the city of love.

"What kind of thing do you like doing?" he asked, as they made their way down to the ground floor.

"As a tourist?" she asked.

He nodded and watched her tilt her head to the side for a moment. Her oval face lit up in the sunlight and made him want to reach out to stroke her cheek and find out if it was as soft as it looked.

"I have no idea," she admitted. "I've never really been a tourist in a place like this. I just want to see stuff."

It was his turn to think hard for a moment, but it wasn't that difficult. Paris had a lot of famous landmarks of different types, things to see, and places to experience. And there were a lot of restaurants too. They could spend all day and see but a fraction of it. Maybe even a whole week and still not take it all in.

With neither of them having a major preference, they found the nearest metro station and picked the nearest landmark they both liked the sound of, which was Notre Dame. They both knew it could only be seen from the outside right now, but even that was kind of cool given the fire they'd heard about.

"Did you know that some of our kind helped build this place when it was originally made?" Alia asked.

"Really?" Rich's eyes were wide.

"Yeah. I think they're helping with the reconstruction too, but we have to be careful not to make it too obvious that it's all magic. Got to take our time so it seems believable to all you amagical folks."

"It really makes you wonder what would change in the world if we did all know about magic and it could come out into the open."

"If everyone was like you, Natalie, and Lucas, it would probably be fine. But some humans are like Daven. It's bad enough when one of our kind does something like that, but when one of your kind does it, it can be even worse."

"I'm sorry," Rich offered. He could see the pain in Alia's eyes. He didn't know what memory she was haunted by, but it was clearly something that bothered her and he didn't need to know anything else.

"It's okay. Let's go around this thing and I'll point out what we made. And then we can go find some lunch."

"Sounds perfect." Rich knew he'd have agreed to about anything in that moment and it wouldn't have mattered. They were together and enjoying a new city. It was all sights he'd never seen either, and after all the time he'd spent in the last few months working hard on getting their glasses working, and then everything with Daven and trying to work out how to break the curse on Lucas, he hadn't stopped and done anything fun in so long.

He had the glasses on him, so he put them on to see what they knew about Notre Dame. They didn't tell him anything major. If he looked down and around him, it tried to overwhelm him with information on the masses of people nearby, a flaw still with the system.

They'd only ever tested it in relatively quiet areas. In a busy city such as Paris, they were in need of some fine-tuning. The view was covered in far too much writing, and it struggled to keep up and process everything. Question marks appeared where it couldn't find the information fast enough, then there would be more flickering and distracting visuals as it filled it in.

Rich could see why it had been too much for Natalie on a few occasions, though she'd done a good job of using them for the team in the heat of battles and difficult situations.

Sadly, Lucas had hardly gotten to experience the wonder of his creation and how it worked. He'd been cursed too soon to get to use them, and Rich thought he was losing too much of his mind now to improve the project even if he could have gripped a tool.

He took the glasses back off again and put them back in his pocket, letting Alia tell him anything she wanted unhindered. Despite never having been a tourist in the city, she knew a lot about what her kind had done. She had a good memory and mind for all sorts of information.

By the time they were ready for lunch, Rich was even more impressed with the young elf.

Natalie sighed and rubbed her eyes. She'd been trying to work out this press release for hours and thought she might go mad if she looked at it anymore. She'd mostly offered to stay behind and work to give Alia and Rich some time alone together to see if something might develop between the pair. They had so many people waiting to know about their tech now that she had to do something, though.

On top of that, Lucas was still not quite himself. He'd woken enough to drink and eat a little and mumble incoherently before falling asleep again.

It was time she got herself some lunch. She'd left him curled up on the sofa in the little living room area and she was set up at one end of the dining table where she could see him. She went over to him now.

He'd wriggled a lot and seemed to be coming out of his sedated state.

She stroked him and called his name a few times. When

he didn't stir or move much more than a few twitches, she stood again.

"Don't stop," he protested. "That was nice. I feel a bit achy and rough, though."

"I'm not surprised. You're probably dehydrated and hungry. You've been out cold for two days pretty much."

"Two days!" He sat up, and his cat eyes winced at the pain that moving gave him. "What happened?"

"We needed to get a vet to approve you so we could fly. We're in Paris."

Lucas jumped down from the sofa and went to the tall window on one side of the apartment. He jumped up on a small table to be able to look outside and see down into the city.

"You all suck, you know that, right?"

"You know that we're just trying to save you and keep us all from having our memories wiped, right?"

He sighed. "I feel like shit. You must have given me loads of sedatives."

"We did. You were talking as a cat in places we needed you not to."

Again Lucas winced and nodded, this time from under-standing.

"It wasn't too bad. I brought your passport with us so we can keep trying to get you back to human form and you can still get back." Natalie sat near him, hoping he under-stood they were trying to do their best by him.

"Thank you… Now, tell me there's some good food for me in this place somewhere? Paris is meant to be the city of love and food, and I'm not finding the former in cat form, so I definitely want the latter."

Natalie laughed and got up to go see what she could rustle up. They'd grabbed some food from the nearest convenience store the afternoon before, and a few of the options were cat friendly.

He followed her through to the kitchen and jumped up on the counter.

"I'm pretty sure I should be shooing you off there," Natalie commented as she moved around him to get to the fridge.

"If I ever lose my mind entirely, feel free. But while I can still talk to you, I can sit where I like."

She wasn't going to argue, and she wasn't going to point out that his words were no longer as clear as they once were. They sounded more like meows sometimes than they did words. Hearing something like that would make him worry even more.

It was nice to be with Lucas and make food and for a while forget about everything but enjoying life. While they ate, she told him everything they'd learned about the werewolf they were pursuing and what they needed to make happen.

"What happened with the vet?" Lucas asked once they'd talked about everything else he had missed. "Did Rich bribe him or something to give us the paperwork? Please tell me that it was just a bribe?"

Natalie shrugged as she picked up their empty plates and made herself busy suddenly.

"We didn't go with him. He said it would be better for his friend if it was just him and you and you've been fine, so I'm sure that whatever happened it was nothing awful."

Lucas looked at her and Natalie could feel herself being

studied, but she did her best to focus on the menial task in front of her and not react with any obvious guilt.

"Okay, but I'm not going to forget the three of you drugging me. You let the elf shoot me."

"It was a tranquilizer dart," Natalie replied, protesting the insinuation.

"She still shot me with it."

"I know. And she didn't miss while you were running away and trying to jump up at a door. You should have seen the look of concentration on her face. She knew she wasn't going to miss you. It was almost scary."

"I guess we'd all better not piss her off."

Natalie nodded, agreeing with the full sentiment. If nothing else, Alia knew how to wield a gun.

CHAPTER TEN

Looking at her three companions, Alia wondered how they had ever thought they could survive in the magical world. Natalie was wearing the glasses again and Lucas was riding in Rich's arms as they walked along a busy Paris street toward the main enforcer headquarters for the city and, incidentally, the country.

"I don't know why you didn't just let me put you in the carrier," Rich grumbled when they had walked another block and Lucas was yet again wriggling.

"You know, he could walk. He has feet," Alia pointed out.

"She does have a good point. It's not like we're in a hurry." Natalie glanced at her watch. "It's not far from here and we still have fifteen minutes before our appointment. We're going to be early."

Rich shrugged and dumped Lucas on the ground. Stifling a grin, Alia watched as Lucas huffed, raised his head and tail in the air in much the way an imperious cat does, and stalked ahead of them.

It made Alia chuckle, and she didn't even try to keep it quiet. These three were dorks, but they were adorable dorks in their own way. She had no idea how they were going to help apprehend a wanted werewolf criminal when she looked at them like this, but then she remembered how the same three had helped her liberate a warehouse full of slaves and stop a powerful magic-wielding elf.

"Are there werewolf enforcers as well?" Rich asked a moment later. "Is this going to be like human police keeping humans in order?"

"Maybe… It's more complicated than that. Most enforcers are elven or centaur. Whichever races lend themselves to either detective work or having enough magic to outmatch powerful magic users. You can't enforce rules if you're not capable of doing so."

"Sounds like it's a dangerous job. Having to make sure you're more powerful than those you're trying to police. With humans, it's so much simpler. Most of us can't do anything particularly deadly and if we can because we've been trained then they can be controlled by the other people who trained with them. Unless you believe the conspiracy theories anyway."

"Most of the time enforcers don't have a tough time either. The average criminal magic user is still a teenage elf trying a spell for the first time and making a total mess of it and being more public than they ought to be. Or some elf, using magic to hold up a store and steal a bunch of food for their family. It's no different than guns."

None of them could argue with that. Alia appreciated that they were trying to get their heads around her world, however. Maybe there was hope for them after all.

The enforcers' office was a grand building in the way that most of the buildings in the center of Paris were. Everything was tall, and the entrances to the buildings were framed with columns. It made them seem more imposing, but it was also beautiful in its own way. It was more appealing to the eye than many of the enforcer buildings in the US.

Alia led the way in, noticing that Lucas held back, no longer quite so haughty as they all trooped inside.

A reception desk stood at the far end of a large marble-floored lobby. It had enough offices inside it that there were enforcers coming and going all over the place, most often in pairs and almost always in deep discussions about something.

"It's a bit like being in the lobby of the main CIA building," Natalie said.

"You've been there?" Rich replied.

"No…" She blinked, and Alia was pretty sure that she had lied. "I've seen it on TV. You know, in one of those thriller shows."

It was a strange thing to not want to talk about, but given what Natalie had told Alia of her upbringing and how much she resented her wealthy parents, Alia guessed Natalie probably didn't want to seem special. It wasn't easy being different.

Trying to give her friend some space and feeling gratitude at knowing something the others might not, Alia strode up to the desk and informed the receptionist who they were and who they were meant to be there to see.

"We're a little early," Lucas added as he jumped up onto the edge of the desk.

The receptionist gasped, but more out of surprise than shock that a cat had spoken to her.

"That's fine. They have their own office on the fifth floor. Head to the elevator on your right and when you exit it, head left, down a corridor and the second door on your right."

Alia thanked the receptionist and picked up Lucas so that he couldn't scare someone who might be even more jumpy and cast a spell as a reflex.

"Are you trying to get yourself double cursed?" she asked him once they were on the inside of the small metal box and Natalie was punching the right button.

"I thought it was funny. I'm a cat because some elf wanted to enslave us, and no one seems to know how to get me back to a human. If I can't at least have some fun with this before I turn back or stop being able to talk then what is the point in life?"

"He's not wrong," Rich allowed.

Alia glared at him. Lucas didn't need any encouragement. She was back to wondering how these three survived being in the magical world at all.

By the time they reached the doorway they'd been directed to, a tall elf was standing waiting for them. This must be enforcer Philip Dupont.

"The group from the US?" he asked as he looked them over, his head held a little higher.

The disdain on his face was clear as he took in the two humans but the moment he noticed Alia and his gaze flicked to the features that marked her as another of his species his frown deepened. The cat in her arms made it even worse.

"We don't allow pets in here. Please—"

"Good thing we don't have any pets with us then," Lucas interrupted. He jumped down and hurried past the enforcer and into the office behind him. "Is this your office?"

If the elf had looked like he didn't want them there before, he was positively angry now. His fists clenched as he turned to follow the tabby cat.

Alia loved the lack of fear her friends had when it could piss off someone who clearly thought too much of themselves.

Alia hurried after him, also squeezing past and through the door, although she bumped him a little. "Lucas is the person who made the glasses I understand you've been told about."

"Before he was cursed, anyway," Natalie added and motioned for their host to follow with a broad grin on her face.

Dupont looked as if he didn't appreciate being offered the courtesy of his own office, but he couldn't stand out in the hallway on principle alone.

Lucas had already jumped up onto one of the chairs in front of a large mahogany desk and sat.

Dupont recovered and strode toward the other side of the desk. "I was informed of these glasses of yours. They can see information. Things we cannot?"

"Yes. They tap into many databases in all sorts of places and networks, and they feed that information to the wearer." Natalie smiled, pointing to them.

"I would like to see." The enforcer held out his hand to take the glasses, but she shook her head and pulled back.

"Nope. I'm sorry. We can't let you. There are investors backing our product and I have a responsibility and legal requirement to them to not allow our prototype to be touched, tampered with, or otherwise put at risk. I cannot let you have them."

Once again, the enforcer frowned. Alia wondered what magical abilities this elf might have. Was there a chance they were going to pick up another curse for one of them?

"Why don't you tell us about Francisco? That's why we're here. How did he achieve the destruction and removal of so much evidence?"

Although Alia was trying to make things better, she found this made the enforcer even more surly and he lifted his chin a fraction higher again.

"This is something that may be hard for you to understand, and it is clear that you are all out of your depth. Amagical humans with nothing but some fancy technology going against one of the greatest criminal masterminds the magical world has ever seen. I do not know what will be suggested next."

"That may be, but we've been asked to try and find him for you." Natalie leaned forward again. "We don't want to engage him in battle or anything. We're just going to track him down and then call you to do the rest. Think of us as the trackers. We're not going to do anything more if we don't have to."

Natalie's words soothed the guy, and he nodded and sat back. A moment later he put his elbows on the desk and steepled his fingers together.

"Francisco is no ordinary werewolf. He possesses an ancient lineage that was crossed with the dryads. They have sway over certain old magics that make it very easy for them to manipulate certain things in certain ways and he has grown up with a strong affinity for these things."

"He charms people and they find it harder to resist than normal," Alia finished for the enforcer. He was making excuses. Elves were resistant to dryad charms and many other similar magics. It's why they made good enforcers.

Dupont didn't hide his annoyance at being interrupted. Over the course of the next half hour, he reluctantly told them everything and answered their questions about the current situation. It was a little like drawing blood out of a stone as the enforcer tried to keep certain information to himself regarding the stupidity of his own colleagues, but what he didn't tell them, they could piece together well enough.

Dupont pulled out a file and showed them a list of every case that had been tampered with or blown up by Francisco's actions. Alia let him have his say and didn't tell him that they'd hacked the system and looked through it all already.

He kept it brief and offered them the small dossier to keep. "Recovering as much of this as possible is our primary goal. Catching Francisco is secondary. Is that clear?"

"Doesn't matter much to us. We're just finding this guy for you, right?" Alia grinned and got up.

For a second no one else moved, and she wondered if she'd forgotten something, but Dupont got to his feet, seeming to be frustrated that he had to fight gravity to do so.

"With any luck, you'll be back in your own country soon and we'll be able to put all this behind us."

"I think we'd like that as well," Natalie replied, her arms folded across her chest. After she'd refused to let him try on the glasses, he hadn't spoken another word directly to Natalie, and he'd acted as if she weren't there as he shepherded them out of the office.

CHAPTER ELEVEN

The entire team was sitting at a table outside a café. Rich had a file open in front of him, still trying to decide whether this was worth their time and worrying about Lucas and getting him back to normal.

All they had to go on to begin their werewolf hunt were several recent sightings of Francisco and some speculation and rumors of where he might be staying. In case they got lucky, they'd opted to get lunch at a restaurant near these locations.

It was something they should be able to narrow down. It just required a little investigation, and Rich knew they could do it. Something about beating Daven and helping all the enslaved magical beings had shown him that his friends and he were capable of more than they realized.

He stroked Lucas while he looked over maps of Paris and the sightings and combined it with information on local events that might be the sort of thing the werewolf would attend. Natalie had pointed out that he was often seen at big, wealthy social events before a job, or that the victims often met him at those sorts of things.

Getting into such highbrow places was something Rich feared they'd never be able to do. They were the kind of events that it wasn't easy to get an invite to even if you were relatively wealthy. He wondered if this was how the private detectives in his favorite crime novels felt at the beginning of each series when they were struggling to make ends meet because they were down on their luck. Did they have to talk their way into events and get clients to pay strange bills?

As they were preparing to leave and try something else, Rich said, "I think there's two events that it's worth going to or trying to get into in some way. Staff, or otherwise. Maybe Dupont could help get us into them."

Natalie sat bolt upright and stared across the road, gripping the arms of her chair. "No need. Francisco is now coming out of a building over there. The glasses have picked up on him and that he's a wanted criminal."

"Really?" Rich turned to look until Alia smacked his arm.

"Don't make it too obvious," she hissed.

"I can't see him anyway. Are you sure he's there?"

"The guy is a master of disguise and he likes to blend in unless he's flaunting himself. He's a con artist. You aren't always going to recognize him. That's why he's so good."

Rich frowned. He didn't like having something like that pointed out to him. Not when he should have thought of it himself.

Making a mental note to get more of the glasses made

as soon as they could so everyone could have a set and see the same information, Rich gathered his stuff.

"Lead the way," he suggested as everyone else followed suit. "We should tail him and see if we can work out where he's going and what he's up to. Let the enforcers know where he is."

Natalie was already walking down the street with Alia guiding her so she could ignore people closer to her and the information the glasses gave.

Instead of running along beside Rich, Lucas pawed at his friend's leg to be carried. He had told Rich that, in the busier areas of Paris, he didn't like walking along the ground. There were too many people who didn't notice a cat at their feet or were simply in too much of a hurry.

"It's going to get really tiring carrying you around everywhere," Rich complained as he picked him up yet again.

"I don't like it either. You're smelly this close. I'm a cat now and people smell really strong. And it's not that comfortable being picked up. I'd rather sit on your shoulders or something."

Rich lifted Lucas to his shoulders and hoped it was easier to carry the cat that way. They were all getting fed up with the whole situation and having Lucas stuck like this. It would have tested any friendship.

They wove through the crowds after Natalie, who was doing her best to follow Francisco through the city and past several major monuments. He took them across a large bridge and around a few more bends, and with each turn, Rich wondered how Natalie was managing to track anything. This werewolf could move fast and he clearly didn't want anyone following him.

A couple of times, Rich wondered if Francisco had spotted them. The werewolf glanced back now and then, but he didn't seem to be bothered by them if he had noticed.

After walking around the city the day before with Alia as well, Rich's feet soon started to ache, and having Lucas on his shoulders grew more and more uncomfortable. "We're not getting him cornered anywhere any time soon," he suggested. "We should let the enforcers know where he is, and they can pick him up and challenge him on everything."

Natalie continued walking, not even glancing at him. "Maybe, but we don't know if they'll get here in time or if he'll slip away."

"Do we need to care? They asked us to find him. We found him. And it didn't take us long, either."

"Technically, they asked us to help apprehend him and return the evidence needed for the other crimes too. I am pretty sure we're meant to be doing more than just point him out. I *want* to do more than just point him out." Alia steered Natalie around a street vendor and kept her out of the road.

"Lost him again," Natalie reported as they reached an intersection. She walked forward, looking this way and that as she tried to find Francisco again. After a minute, she added, "Nope. He's gone and I don't know where."

"Let me try," Lucas suggested and jumped down off Rich's shoulders. He ran ahead of them, trying to smell out

Francisco, but it wasn't as easy as it looked in the movies, and there were far too many people in this busy area of Paris.

Within another few minutes, Lucas had given up as well. "I can find his scent here and there," he explained. "Werewolves smell a fair bit, but I don't know what direction he went in or what he did beyond this point. Can't find a trail."

"We did what we could. If we've found him once, we can find him again." Alia scooped Lucas up and let him nuzzle into her for a moment.

"Let's go back to the apartment," Rich proposed. "Put what we've got into a tracker and work out where to try next." Rich led the way, wondering if there was a coding solution to their problem. Sometimes computer systems could study books or habits well enough that they could make surprisingly accurate predictions.

None of them talked much on their way back. After spotting Francisco so soon, it had felt like they might get their mission done quickly. Despite the unrealistic nature of that hope, they were all disappointed.

By the time they got back to the apartment block, Rich's feet were aching and he was ready to collapse into a chair and let his brain do the work. There was something about this werewolf. He'd never seen anyone else command that sort of presence. Rich looked forward to trying to find him at a party or something like that. Something where Rich would get to see the werewolf face to face, maybe even talk to him.

They arrived at the apartment, and Natalie breezed in.

Lucas padded over to the sofa and sat while Alia went to get a drink.

They were all exhausted, but Rich was going to sit down and get a computer to help him. After all, that was what he was good at.

CHAPTER TWELVE

Alia sighed as she flung herself down in the seat beside Rich and stared over at him.

"Still working on that computer program?" she asked. He was putting together the last touches and feeding in the last of the information they had on Francisco's crimes and how he operated.

"It's finished. I think. Now it just needs to analyze the information and then spit out a prediction on where he'll be next." Rich grinned. It had taken him three days of solid working with Natalie helping him out here and there, and it was still more crude than he liked, but Alia, Lucas, and Natalie hadn't gotten any further using their method in the same time.

Sitting back, he waited for it to run and focused on Alia. "You still intent on putting this guy behind bars?"

"Yes. His crimes are awful. He's a vile excuse for a living creature and the people he has scammed and the evidence he took. Werewolves are some of the worst of the fantastical races alive. And I can't see them make things worse for our kind and abuse their strength or charms. He goes behind bars and we're going to make it happen."

Rich nodded.

"If that thing spits out a place then you can check it out without me," Natalie put in. "I'm done. I've been all over Paris in the last four days and I am not ready to see another sight, eat another rich meal or browse another expensive shop full of things I can't afford. You're on your own."

"Noted." Alia retrieved the glasses and took them to Rich. "Looks like it'll just be me and you."

"I didn't say that I wasn't coming." Lucas came closer, flicking his tail.

"You can stay here. The last time I took you out, I ended up carrying you," Rich replied. "On my shoulders."

"And I'm not going to bring you either. Natalie or I have ended up doing the same while Rich has been coding." Alia folded her arms as Lucas sat and tilted his head sideways.

"You can stay here with me. I'll get some more tuna and we'll watch TV reruns while I give you head scritches." Natalie picked up Lucas and took him to the sofa.

At first, it looked like Lucas was going to object to being hauled to the TV and given little choice about it, but he relaxed into Natalie's arms and started purring. It made Alia grin. They needed to get him turned back into a human, but it was kind of cool having a cat around that could talk.

Rich pulled Alia's attention back to his computer. "Okay, this thing is starting to narrow down locations and run stats on likely places we'll see Francisco and times of day."

She followed his gaze to a readout on the computer that was listing places and percentages of likelihood that the werewolf would be there. It began as a small list without much surety, but as it compared more and more information and pulled up itineraries and schedules from people and cross-compared data, it became more and more solid.

"Is that thing using illegal information?" she asked when she noticed the calendars of wealthy people being scanned.

"Only if we sell the information or try to use it to sell something to them…" Rich didn't sound sure of himself.

"The answer is that it's a gray area," Natalie supplied from over by the sofa.

"I didn't exactly have permission, but we'll delete the data when we're done, and we're kind of using it to keep them safe. They'll also never know." Rich grinned and Alia couldn't help but smile back as the program fixed on a single place and offered it as a possible destination for their werewolf.

"Good. I definitely wasn't going to tell anyone." Alia pointed to the name of the bar. "Looks like we have a place to head. I'll get my coat."

They got up at the same time, and Alia felt a small thrill of delight at getting to go explore more of Paris in the evening. In some ways, it was a shame she didn't have a job at the place. Wealthy people were some of the easiest to steal from if you knew what you were doing.

It took her a little longer to get ready than she'd implied. Alia knew better than anyone that to get into some of the best places in a city like Paris, you had to look the part.

Rich had the same idea and came back out of his room wearing tailored pants, shiny shoes, a nice shirt, and a far neater hairstyle than he'd had before.

"Good, you look the part too." She grabbed his arm and decided they were going to act like a couple to get into the place at least.

He grabbed a suit jacket and waved to Natalie and Lucas. "I've always wanted to do this."

Natalie grinned at Alia and waved before returning to her show. "Have fun, you two. Message me if you find him and need backup."

Rich also grabbed the glasses and put them on. They were bulkier than suited Rich's face and detracted from his handsome look a little, but if Francisco was in disguise again they would appreciate the extra help identifying him.

With a wave of a credit card the enforcers had provided, Rich was ready.

"Do you think this counts as a business expense?" she asked as they caught a taxi. It struck Alia as a strange way of thinking about it, but he was their target and this was a cost of trying to catch him. She'd never worked for anyone in this capacity before. Normally she was tasked with getting an item, or she took something she thought she might be able to sell.

This was hunting some*one*, and this was also for the other side of the law.

All around them, people were speaking French, but now and then they heard someone speak English, usually with a British accent. They had to join a small queue for the bar, where a bouncer checked that he liked the look of people and kept it from getting too crowded inside.

Unsurprisingly to Alia, some people got to walk straight in, bypassing the line of people waiting. It was something Alia had always wondered about. The magical world had the same class hierarchy as well. If you had wealth you were treated better. Sometimes, if you looked like you did, you also could get away with it, but neither Alia nor Rich had any belongings quite that high-end.

If she'd been willing to take the risk, she could have stolen some clothes and accessories for them that would have given them the edge they might need, but the shops were all shut and it was too late now.

The queue wasn't long and moved fairly quickly, though. Plenty of people were coming and going and they were soon being shown to a table near the bar and handed menus.

"They actually serve snails," Alia exclaimed a few seconds later.

"Is that what you want?"

She shook her head. She didn't want to waste the opportunity to have a good meal. Instead, she ordered what sounded like a fancy burger and fries and a glass of red wine.

With Rich able to put it on the credit card and both of them trying to look the part, she didn't worry about the expense. She didn't get to eat out as often as she'd like, and she wanted to enjoy it while she could.

"So, do you think he's here yet?" she asked as they both surreptitiously looked around and sized up the other patrons. The many tables were spread out in an open space, and plants, low walls, and decorations kept anyone from feeling too close to another group. Most diners were lost in conversation or busy poring over their menus.

There were a lot of couples, tourists probably in Paris to savor the romance, but there were also a few larger groups and two people each on their own sitting at tables near the sides out of the way. One was working on his laptop, and another was reading and taking his meal slowly as he enjoyed the book and the food.

Alia envied the latter man. His head was almost bald and his skin was brown and wrinkled from time. He looked as if he'd seen many summers and had taken delight and memories from all of them. For a moment, she wished she could see into his mind and what he was thinking of and reading, but he wasn't the werewolf they were looking for and that meant she had to move on.

At first, Alia ignored the couples, assuming that Francisco would be alone or part of a large group where he was trying to scam multiple people, but none of the other groups had anyone in them who looked as if they fit the bill.

For a few seconds, she studied a group of wealthy men and women at the bar. They were talking about something but appeared to be waiting for someone and almost impatient about it. None of them was the werewolf, however. They were all too short.

Once she'd ascertained that he wasn't among the groups, she studied the couples. Rich didn't say too much to her as he looked around and moved the glasses on his face.

"It's fascinating how much information these things can

find," Rich mused, looking over the same group she'd studied. "There's an incredibly wealthy elf over there."

Alia had noticed her own kind before anything else. "There's another five elves in the room."

Rich looked at her and she flashed him a smile as their food arrived. They both tucked in, looking up now and then to see if Francisco had arrived.

They were both beginning to get antsy and wonder whether the computer program had been wrong when more people arrived. Alia glanced over them, but none of them seemed to be the werewolf. There were a few men, and some of them were tall enough, but if they were Francisco Alia couldn't tell.

A couple of seconds later, Rich almost dropped his fork.

"He's here. It actually worked. Francisco is here." Rich's mouth was open and he was staring toward the bar.

Alia tried to follow his gaze but all she saw was the same group of wealthy patrons. They appeared to have their missing person now, and they had all gathered around a single person. It took her several more seconds to realize that was who Rich was talking about.

Her mouth fell open like Rich's had. Francisco looked completely different than he had the day before. It was almost impossible not to stare.

"I'm going to go talk to him." Rich got up and left his food behind.

Alia shrugged and sat back to watch the train wreck.

CHAPTER THIRTEEN

Although others were talking to Francisco, Rich could already see that the conversation wasn't necessarily going in the werewolf's direction. A female elf was charmed a little and clearly the target of the conman's plans that evening, but then a male elf arrived and pushed past Rich to get to the group.

It had initially appeared as if the group of socialites had been waiting for Francisco, but from the way this elf apologized for being late as they all moved off toward a table and left the werewolf behind, Rich got the impression that he'd slotted himself into a group because they were there and wealthy.

As the party of people moved away, Francisco frowned and sat himself down at the bar. He ordered a drink and surveyed the room in much the way Rich had.

This was his moment. Rich continued to the bar. "Never fun going for the girl and finding another guy has beaten you to the punch," he offered. "Commiserations on me."

Francisco raised an eyebrow but nodded and accepted the drink.

"You saw that?"

"I was considering talking to her as well. Let's just say you saved me the embarrassment with the elf." Rich looked away as he said the last word, knowing that it wasn't something he should throw around, but it would make it clear that he was aware of the magical world even if he wasn't able to do anything magical.

After ordering his own drink, Rich sat on the bar stool beside Francisco. When he looked back up, the werewolf was appraising him. Rich had to fight not to shudder and wondered if the whole evening was going to be like this.

After a moment the werewolf grinned again. "I'm Peter. I'm here for a few days on business. It is easy to be distracted by a pretty face, is it not? It seems you have equally good taste in the finer things of life. Cheers."

Rich raised his glass in response to Francisco's. "I'm Rich," he returned, not even thinking of lying until it was too late. "Also here on business. Not sure how long I'll be here. But that's the way it goes sometimes."

"Then it seems for tonight at least we are brothers in arms. Left to nurse our hearts and drinks and try not to think of our work."

Rich chuckled at the words. It was a funny way of saying it and the werewolf spoke with a flamboyant tone, but it was clear he knew how to talk to someone and put them at ease.

For the next hour, the two of them talked about life, women, and not always being lucky. They exchanged stories of crushes and romantic flames who turned them down. Francisco was self-deprecating but also funny, and before long Rich was wondering how this guy could be a criminal.

The time slipped by and he continued talking to Francisco until Alia came up to the bar on one side of him, acting like they didn't know each other. She ordered another glass of wine. She caught her foot on his stool as she turned and made sure he'd seen her.

It reminded him that he was not there to drink but to get information from Francisco and figure out how to get this guy arrested and where the evidence he'd taken was. He needed to start asking more questions, not talking about women.

He drew a blank for a moment as he stared at his drink. Was this his fifth, or his sixth? He'd lost track somewhere along the way. Rich tried to concentrate and work out what to say.

"So what business do you do?" he blurted, interrupting something he'd stopped following anyway. At the same time, he looked over at Alia. She had gone back to their table, and he saw an empty dessert bowl along with an empty bottle of wine.

Francisco paused, a brief frown appearing on his face as he studied Rich for a moment. "We *have* probably talked about women enough, haven't we? They can be a terrible distraction."

"A huge distraction. Some of them even get you cursed. Or your friends." Rich glanced at Alia again.

This time Francisco followed his gaze and looked out at the tables of people for a moment as well.

"I am a software engineer," Rich replied. "The exact

kind of work that women either love or hate. No middle ground. Tell me that you do something that's a bigger hit?"

"I… can't say I do. Accountant. I like numbers and I'm good with them. Not something a lot of women enjoy hearing about, however."

"Accountant? You don't strike me as anything near so dull. Come on, there must be more to what you do than just crunch numbers. You've got to be here in Paris for a better reason. It's the city of love and we've talked about women all evening. Tell me you have a good purpose for being here." Rich swung his glass, ready to raise it again, almost as if he was challenging Francisco to give him a reason to toast something.

"We each are as we each are, and we divulge what we see fit. I am an accountant, and I help the wealthy with their finances."

"Helping the wealthy…" Rich sighed. "Then at least one of us gets to rub shoulders with the big players. Let me guess. They don't always appreciate your help. See what they have to pay you and feel as if it wasn't worth the cost?"

"Something like that, yes." Francisco sat up a little straighter. "I feel that I have drunk more than I intended, and I have work tomorrow as I'm sure you do as well. Goodnight, Rich. Perhaps we will meet again in the future."

"Goodnight…" Rich realized he had forgotten the name the werewolf had given him as an alias. "See you around. Perhaps another evening."

"Unlikely." Francisco clapped him on the shoulder as he went to walk past and left his hand there for a moment, the weight and grip almost showing Rich that this was a powerful person and Rich could be crushed if he wasn't careful. "I don't like being interrupted in my work once I have the bit between my teeth on a project. And I very much will have, here. I might not be good company if we saw each other again. I'm sure you understand."

The werewolf strode away without looking back, but he met Alia's gaze and nodded to her on the way out.

The young elf's eyes went wide before she took a final gulp of her wine and came over to Rich's side. "What happened?" she demanded.

"I think he figured out that I was onto him or something. Worked out that you and me were working together."

Alia exhaled, her teeth gritting as she looked toward the door along with Rich. Francisco was long gone, but that didn't stop the two of them from hoping that he would come back. How could they have found him and let him slip through their fingers again? They were learning nothing except how good a master of disguise he was.

As Rich got up and swayed, Alia took his arm and reminded him to pay the bill. She had to help him get the credit card out and tuck it back before hailing them a taxi.

"Humans. You really can't hold your drink."

CHAPTER FOURTEEN

Amused by the story Alia had told her about the previous night, Natalie walked into Rich's room and opened the curtains.

"Wake up, sleepyhead," she called as the sun shone on his face and made him squint. Lucas jumped up on the bed a second later.

"Does that have to be open?" Rich groaned and tried to shield his eyes with his arm, but Lucas headbutted his hand to get scritches instead.

Rich sat up, still wearing his shirt from the night before.

"Please tell me that you remember what happened last night," Natalie added. A moment later, Alia appeared with an apple and threw it at Rich.

The hungover techie managed to catch it, and he frowned at it.

"It's meant to help soak up the alcohol you consumed." Alia rolled her eyes and then plonked herself down on the end of the bed.

"Okay, out with it. What did he say, what was he like and what do we need to plan for?" Natalie asked. She sat on the stool by the dresser, not wanting to add another to the already crowded bed but impatient to find out what Rich had.

"He was great, actually. Really easy to talk to." Rich tried to buy himself a moment to think back and figure out what had been said.

"Awesome. So you got loads of info?" Natalie folded her arms, her patience worn out by already waiting for the others to think it acceptable to wake Rich up.

"I…" Rich gulped, and Natalie could have sworn at him.

"You were talking to him for *hours*," Alia reminded him, making it clear she was even less impressed than Natalie at finding out the night hadn't gained them much information.

"He told a lot of stories and I'm not sure how true they all were. I'm pretty sure I interrupted him as he was trying to talk to an elf though. Like he was trying to pick out a new target, but someone else showed up and pulled the elf away."

"Oh, that pretty thing with the Gucci purse?" Alia tilted her head to the side, almost as if she was trying to picture the woman.

"Yeah, Francisco was talking to her before I joined him. And he mentioned her a few more times. When I tried to get more out of him, he got funny though. Seemed to be offended that we weren't talking more about women, and then when I pried a little further, he got funny and left." Rich put a hand to his head and winced as he tried to move.

"So it sounds like our only lead is that elf..." Alia got up again and left the room. She came back a moment later with her phone. "Good thing I got a photo of her, isn't it?"

Natalie smiled as Rich continued to look shell-shocked and bit into the apple absentmindedly. It was almost amusing how hungover he was, but they had more work to do. She got the impression that Francisco had done something to Rich. He had a strange look in his eye when he talked about the werewolf and their meeting.

"Did you really just talk about this elf for two hours?" Natalie asked when Alia showed her the picture. The elf was attractive, and clearly had money, but there wasn't anything so special about her that Natalie thought Rich might prefer her over Alia.

"Nah, we only talked about her for a few minutes. Not long at all really. He told wonderful stories of other women and people he'd met." The wistful, almost enchanted look appeared again. She caught Alia's gaze and saw the smirk that crossed her face.

"Is he under some kind of spell?" she asked.

"No, he's just charmed, that's all. It wears off fairly quickly and doesn't do any real harm. It does mean he's going to be less useful around Francisco though." Alia shrugged and got to work trying to find out who the elf was.

"Good to know. I guess we exclude our Mr. Suck Up from any direct contact with our conman from now on."

Alia gave Natalie an apologetic look. "We might want to exclude you too."

"Why?" Natalie folded her arms across her chest.

"Werewolf. If he can charm Rich with his magic, then he can charm you too."

"But not you?"

"It doesn't work anywhere near so well on elves. Which is why his choice of target is a strange one."

"He might love the challenge," Lucas suggested as he got up and jumped off the bed. "If he's as good as they say he is, then this has got to be getting boring for him." The cat padded out of the room.

"Or she has something worth the risk." Alia got up again, and she and Natalie followed Lucas, leaving Rich to get up and sort himself out.

Natalie and Alia went straight to the computers to use an image search to find the elf.

"Here she is," Natalie reported as she pulled up the information. "A socialite by the name of Gabriela Devey."

They both pored over all the information they could find on her, but there wasn't a lot on the general internet. She was an heiress and she loved to live a busy life acting charitable and investing in arts and drama in Europe. Nothing made her look like much of a target, other than she was elven, not that the public information on her said that.

"There's got to be something that she's involved in or owns," Alia mused. "Francisco wouldn't just be after money."

"We might not find it online in an obvious place," Natalie replied. "Do you know anyone who might have an idea if she's involved in anything magical? Or do we need to follow her or talk to people near her to get some idea of what she might be into?"

Alia sat back and tilted her head to the side while Natalie waited. It reminded her that there was still a lot to learn about the magical world. How did a person find out about another or learn anything when so little of the information could be public? They'd gotten used to being able to use the internet and find information or dig into things, but the magical world didn't have easy access at the tap of a button.

"I know a few people who might have some information. But none of them owe me any favors anymore and I don't know what they'd know of someone on another continent. We might get a ping on something though. If Francisco heard info in the US that brought him here, then maybe we can find it from folks in the US too. Let me send some messages."

Natalie nodded and went back to trying to dig into the public information on Gabriela. There wasn't a lot that was definite. She didn't need to do anything for money and she had friends who invited her to events and took her recommendations on all sorts of issues. The rest of her time was spent helping charities.

She was someone that you could admire. It appeared as if she did a lot to help others, but when you looked at how much money she still had and how little of her own money went to charity, it was less impressive. In essence, she was just very good at persuading others that they wanted to part with *their* money for a good cause.

By the time Alia came back, Natalie wasn't sure whether she liked the socialite or not.

Alia sat back down. "Nothing for sure yet, but someone did mention that she had made a strange purchase a couple of years ago. She owns a cemetery here in Paris."

"A cemetery?"

"Yup. Pretty bizarre thing to buy, right?"

"Any explanation on why she bought it?" Natalie asked as she pulled open another browser tab and typed in the cemetery name—the Père Lachaise Cemetery.

There wasn't much information on it, but Alia continued to send messages to people she knew, then fetched her own tablet to keep looking. There had to be something there that was so important.

After a little bit of digging, Natalie found a short press release that stated Gabriela had bought the land to preserve it and to ensure her own ancestors were respected. It gave some wishy-washy statement about the land being under threat and how she couldn't let her family history be at risk, but made no mention of which ancestors were buried there or how Gabriela knew.

"Something was hidden on the land. Or kept in a crypt there," Alia theorized as Natalie came to the same conclusion.

Natalie shuddered as she thought about what that might mean for their next mission. Going to a cemetery and a crypt after dark—she didn't like the sound of that. Although she was tired of traipsing around Paris landmarks and expensive shops, she wasn't wanting to trade that for something as creepy as a crypt, especially since finding out that the undead really were a thing.

"So there's possibly something magical on this piece of land?" Rich asked when he appeared and they explained everything to him.

"Yeah. And Gabriela might not even know where or what it is."

"So we've got a possible target although we don't know the specific item?" Natalie tried to wrap her head around it as everyone looked at Alia to explain.

"There's a bunch of magical folks buried in the cemetery. Almost guaranteed. They'll have artifacts with them. Magical items. There's almost definitely somebody buried on the land with something valuable. If Francisco has worked out that there's something on the land he wants he could be trying to work out if Gabriela has found it."

"Or if it's even there," Rich pointed out.

"Nah, he knows it's there or he wouldn't be bothering at all." Alia tilted her head to the side again but didn't explain what she was thinking.

"If there's all these magical artifacts in the place, how did no one realize it was all full of magical people?" Natalie asked. "Are there a lot more of you than we've realized?"

"Yes, and no. There will be normal people buried there as well," Alia replied, sitting up again. "Things haven't always been so closed off, especially in other cultures. People talk of magic in your history for a reason, and some of the artifacts will be objects that confer things like protection to amagicals we wanted to protect or care for. Maybe even sold to wealthy amagicals."

"Then what changed? Why is everything hiding now?" Lucas, sitting on the rug at their feet, swished his tail.

"It's something that just happened. Shit happens." Alia picked up her phone again and got up as if she had more messages to send.

Rich raised his eyebrows and looked at Natalie. Shrugging, Natalie tried to think through what could have caused such a reaction. It was probably best to let the young elf go, she decided. They still had a lot to learn. Alia would tell them when she was ready.

CHAPTER FIFTEEN

With few other leads and not much coming from her contacts in the US, Alia could only think of one other way to get information. The problem was that it wasn't something she wanted to do.

There were bound to be other weres who knew something. Someone like her could always find out what they needed. But it meant going to the parts of Paris where the weres had their Unplaces, and as an elf, it wasn't a great place to go.

If she didn't, though, they were stalled out on a lead on Francisco. The enforcers clearly didn't have a clue, and if Alia didn't help recover all the evidence for the other cases, so many weres would walk free. That made going into the were community even more dangerous.

She couldn't think of a better solution, though. She would have to do her best to guide her friends through a visit and hope that by having humans with her and letting them appear to take the lead, no one would give her any trouble.

The elf went back to Rich, Natalie, and Lucas. All three of them were looking through a database of important people buried at the cemetery.

As soon as Alia walked in, Natalie looked up at her. The woman's eyes practically begged her to have an alternative.

"I think we should go to the were community and see if we can find out what they know. We know Francisco came here to get evidence to free a bunch of them, and then something kept him here and made him go after Gabriela. So there's a good chance there's a rumor in the were community that caught his interest."

Rich sat back, looking as if he was considering the idea, but she'd seen the relief in the way he relaxed as well. He was as grateful to be stopping as Natalie was. "Sounds dangerous if he's helping them," he suggested, picking up on one of Alia's fears right away.

"Well, we're definitely not letting you handle talking to the locals for sure. But Natalie is likely to be able to get information out of them. I think we should give her the glasses and Lucas can sniff around with you while I go with Natalie and try and figure out what artifact Francisco might be after."

"No arguments from me." Natalie got up and fetched the glasses.

"At some point, we're really going to have to make another set of those," Rich replied, but he also got up and fetched his jacket.

"As soon as I'm not a cat and I have thumbs again, I'll make you another one. And me one too. And then we'll figure out how to make something the investors can be happy with that we can sell."

They took a taxi halfway and then got out to walk the rest of the way. She didn't want to run the risk of talking to the wrong taxi driver and getting herself in any more trouble for any other reason right now. The four of them entered the Unplace on foot, Alia holding Lucas and hanging back.

Now that they had been to several different Unplaces and Natalie and Rich had been given a chance to modify the glasses code, they also picked up on any Unplace that was more widely known in the magical community, which meant Natalie could guide them inside.

She took a right and walked toward what appeared to be a fence around an old building. As she went through it, the illusion rippled for a moment and let all of them know it wasn't real.

Grinning at how dazed Rich still looked, Alia followed with Lucas in her arms. As soon as she was through, the smell hit her. She almost bumped into Natalie, who had stopped with her mouth wide open.

Ahead of them was a strip of tarmac that ended roughly a hundred yards in front of them, getting progressively more broken and worn out until it became nothing but dirt. Beyond that was what looked like a village of wooden houses, nothing but dirt lanes between them and the hustle and bustle of weres as they went about their lives.

When Rich also came through and did bump into Natalie, she recovered enough to step forward and get moving again. It was a relief and Alia exhaled and relaxed, tucking herself in behind the other woman while they approached.

Already people stared at them. Alia was able to identify

several types of different were creatures and guessed the glasses were doing the same for Natalie. They were mostly, but not all, weres. Other magical folk were scattered among them, and enough humans that their group wouldn't be out of place.

"There's so many of them and they're so..." Natalie looked around.

"It's what it is. They like to keep themselves to themselves and they're often insistent on doing things their way," Alia explained. "We should focus on our task and not on what it's like to live here or why."

She motioned for Natalie to lead the way and tried not to think about anything else. She didn't like most weres, and Francisco wasn't selling her on the race so far. She knew she shouldn't judge them, but some memories took a long time to fade.

Lucas jumped from her arms and started sniffing out something.

"Come on, Rich. Let's leave these two ladies to talk to whoever it is they want to talk to, and we'll go check out the area and see what else is going on here. Think of it as being tourists in yet another city."

"Sounds fantastic," Rich replied, sounding anything but enthused. He continued after the cat and left Alia with Natalie.

"We should look for some kind of restaurant or café. There will be a few somewhere near the center," Alia whispered.

"Sounds good. I'd love to try some local food. And I've got the credit card, too. I doubt it will be as fancy as anything you had last night, but that doesn't mean it won't taste good."

"I doubt it, but we can try and find something decent at least." Alia let Natalie lead the way, knowing the glasses would be giving her more information than she herself would be able to pick up on in a place she wasn't familiar with.

They wove through the streets. Natalie smiled at anyone who looked at her but moved with enough purpose that she didn't appear to be a tourist. It was something Alia had taught her the first day they'd been in Paris: how you moved and whether you appeared to have a destination in mind was what made you appear to either be new to an area or not.

In a place like this, none of them wanted to appear to not belong.

"There's a restaurant." Natalie nodded to a sign that was offering a diner-like experience. In a French Unplace, it seemed a little strange, but Alia had seen buildings more out of place than that.

It was as good a place as any to begin looking for someone or getting information and they couldn't do a worse job than Rich had done with Francisco the evening before.

Letting Natalie lead the way again and pretending to be less interested, Alia used the lack of focus to look around more and take more in.

The diner was clean enough and had a strange mix of French art and food with diner-style tables and layout, almost as if it didn't know what it was trying to be, but it was at least trying to be something different.

A woman came over. Alia guessed she was probably a werewolf, and in a minor pack. She had some swagger, but she wasn't drawing attention to herself either. She was also chewing gum and wearing black from head to foot.

"Table just for you two?" she asked. No love for Alia showed in her expression, and she narrowed her eyes when she seemed to realize Natalie was human.

"No, four. We're hoping to meet some friends here. I don't think they're here yet," Natalie replied.

The waitress put them in a booth near the window. It was strange to be sitting somewhere in the middle of an Unplace in the middle of a city she'd never been in before, but again Alia was determined to make the most of it.

"So, where shall we begin?" Natalie asked, looking around them.

A mixed group of people sat at the table behind Alia, and she noticed one of the men, a young werewolf, catch Natalie's eye and grin before flicking a wink. The young woman gave a shy half-smile and lowered her eyes, playing the response perfectly.

Within a few minutes, he was sitting at their table. Alia was almost forgotten as Natalie flirted and they ate lunch together. It was interesting listening to him talk about the city, and Natalie played the new to the area card perfectly.

"You seem to know so much about this place. We've heard that the city can be a lot of fun at night in lots of different ways, but we're not into the normal tourist sorts of things. I've got a bit of a thing for ghost stories and haunted places. Life can be so dull. Sometimes it's fun to be a little scared." Natalie shrugged her shoulders in an almost apologetic way, an "I like what I like, what are you going to do about it?" response.

He frowned for a moment and then looked back at his friends and leaned over the back of the booth.

"Hey, Henry, where is that place you said was haunted?"

"Oh, there was that house, down by the river. I don't know if it's true or not. Could just be some weretigers making a big deal over nothing." Henry didn't look like he cared much and went back to the conversation he was having.

"What about a graveyard or cemetery?" Natalie pressed. "I've heard there are some impressive ones in Paris. Some elf bought one recently, loads of really old magic users there. If anywhere is likely to have strange things happening, what about somewhere like that."

Their informant shrugged. "No, I don't think so. We don't know any stories from over there. They're the kind of place our packs don't go much."

It was all the information they could get out of the werewolf before he changed the subject and tried to get Natalie to agree to go to a party. She gave him enough encouragement that he stopped insisting and let her end the conversation.

As soon as they'd finished eating, Natalie gave an excuse and they paid the bill and left. It was a disappointing result, but they'd done what they could. If anyone in the pack had known anything Natalie would have got it out of them, but it seemed they knew nothing.

They came out of the diner and she caught the eye of some older men standing and having a conversation. Once again, Natalie tried to work her charm and chat about life, being in Paris, and what a visiting witch and her elf friend might do in the city.

It resulted in an equal amount of nothing, with one exception: one of the women passing by at the right moment warned them that the cemeteries were no place for young folk who didn't know what they were messing with. That often powerful artifacts were hidden in them and it was also the domain of some dangerous folk.

"Thank you for the warning. We try not to worry about rumors unless some specifics are known, though. You know what it's like. Everywhere has its ghost stories. We like to know which ones have some basis. Do you know anything?" Natalie asked.

"Youth." She shook her head and walked away.

The words from Natalie seemed to put off the others near her as well and everyone dispersed. She sighed and Alia felt her pain.

"Well, I tried. Shall we go see if we can find the guys?"

"I think we ought to. Hopefully, they had better luck."

CHAPTER SIXTEEN

It took all of Rich's stamina to keep up with Lucas over the next hour as the cat padded around alleys and back streets in one of the largest Unplaces Alia had ever taken them to. He said he was following some scent, but he'd been leading them through the quieter streets of what felt more like a shanty town than anything else.

The place had some decent houses, but all of them looked as if they had seen better days, and while the people milling around were clearly respectable and hardworking, they didn't look as if any of them had much money either. Here and there Rich caught snippets of conversation, but no one paid him any attention and Lucas drew even less notice.

They walked down a quiet backstreet together, a small road that looped around the back of fenced-off gardens and garages. Lucas came down to ground level to walk beside Rich.

"None of the were creatures here appear to be very

happy or prosperous," Lucas mused after a few seconds. "They're all struggling along. It's as if there's no hope."

"Yeah, and Alia reacted strangely to being here too. Almost as if she knew this was what it would be like. I think some of the magical races aren't taking care of each other."

"It's no different among humans," Lucas pointed out. "We've got areas like this too. But I hadn't expected this among the magical folks. They have magic. Surely that means they can help each other out and give each other what they need?"

"I guess not. Maybe magic isn't something that they all have access to in the same way. Maybe it doesn't matter what race any of us are, there's always greed and unfairness."

"That would be sad. I've always hoped that life can be lived better. That someone knows how to make things more fair and show people what it means to live a good life."

Rich tilted his head to the side, wondering where this deep conversation was coming from. He supposed everything they had seen and learned in the last few weeks was making all of them reevaluate the world.

"I think we have to each decide to be the change," Rich finally offered. "If we work on the bit of the world in front of us and enough people join in, then we'll get there eventually."

"You're probably right, but it's not exactly a quick solution."

"Nothing worth doing ever is."

They lapsed into silence as Lucas focused on the scent

he was following again for a while. It appeared as if they were coming to the edge of the wooden houses and the Unplace when Rich heard his name being called from their right. He glanced that way to see Natalie and Alia joining them.

They spent the next few minutes catching up and discussing what they'd heard.

"So there's definitely something at the cemetery," Rich concluded when he'd heard everything Natalie had learned.

"Yes, but we don't know exactly what or where in the cemetery. And it's not a small area of land." Natalie shrugged and Rich thought for a moment.

They needed another lead and right now they didn't have much of one to go on.

"We could find out more about the elf," he suggested as Lucas took off again toward the end of the block.

The other three followed, although no one wanted to hurry. They had all done a lot of walking lately and their task was feeling futile. Nothing they attempted seemed to give them any results.

Lucas reached the corner of a larger wooden house and the short fence that bordered the front yard and stopped, tail stiff upright and head barely poking around the corner.

He pulled back and looked at his friends.

"He's here. Just a few doors down. Francisco is here. I *thought* I might be able to smell him. Or someone like him."

Rich blinked, surprise making him hesitate. Natalie didn't. She hurried forward to peek around the corner. Everyone hunkered down below the height of the fence so Francisco was less likely to see them and then they waited.

"What's he doing?" Alia asked. She was unable to get past Natalie to see.

"Seems to be talking to someone. Buying something maybe. Hard to tell." Natalie tried to back up, but she bumped into Alia, who elbowed Rich and knocked him over.

He winced at the extra bruises he was going to have as Lucas glared at them.

"I've spent all day following this guy's scent. You had better not scare him off now." Lucas quietly hissed at the end of his words, making it extra clear he was angry and they needed to stop mucking this up.

They switched themselves around, but before Alia could do more than stick her head around the corner, Lucas trotted around them and then he was off.

"Looks like Francisco is on the move," Alia muttered before she hurried around the corner behind Lucas.

Rich sighed as Natalie helped him get back to his feet. Once again, they were rushing around on their feet to follow a werewolf that didn't seem to want to be followed.

Natalie soon caught up to Lucas and Alia who were hot on his heels. The werewolf left the Unplace and headed back into the normal section of Paris. They had to pause briefly around another corner while Lucas kept a lookout and Francisco picked something up.

"If we're going to follow Francisco and not spook him, we need to be careful," Alia reminded them. "He's met Rich now and knows his face, and the four of us look conspicuous."

"He may have picked up on you as well," Rich pointed out. "If I can't follow him directly, then neither can you."

"I wasn't going to either. Someone needs to come with you and keep you out of trouble. Especially now he's charmed you."

Rich opened his mouth to object, but Alia grabbed his arm before he had a chance.

"Keep your phone open and share a location with Natalie," Lucas instructed before he bounded off and Natalie had no choice but to follow.

It was a good idea, and it kept them connected and knowing where they all were while Lucas did most of the work for them. Rich and Alia could be nearby in case trouble came up but also stay *out* of trouble if Francisco did something unexpected or spotted them.

They spent the next half hour traveling through Paris, heading after the werewolf at a distance and using communication with Natalie and the GPS location on her phone.

Although they did their best to keep away, they had a couple of close encounters when Francisco stopped at shops, taking his time, eating pastries, and flirting with anyone he liked the look of. Even trying to keep their distance, taking side roads, and trying to predict the route meant that sometimes Rich and Alia were closer to Francisco than Natalie and Lucas were.

Somehow, they managed not to draw his attention, and the werewolf continued about his business.

When they were still half a mile away, Rich realized they were heading toward the very cemetery that they had been talking about. He showed the map to Alia to get her opinion, and she gave him a grim nod. Whatever it was that the werewolf was after, it was on that land or in a crypt.

Rich texted as much to Natalie and she soon confirmed it. The location of her device was so close now that she must have seen Francisco go into the cemetery.

Rich had also had a fascination with ghost stories while he was a kid and had even visited a few haunted houses and things like that, but he wasn't looking forward to being in a graveyard as the afternoon continued and it got darker. They'd been out so long that there wasn't a massive amount of day left. This could become a spooky nighttime hunt around crypts and gravestones.

As more time went by, it became more and more obvious that Francisco was going to be in the cemetery for a while. He had slowed, and therefore so had Natalie.

"Think we should join them?" Rich asked Alia when he showed her that Natalie was stationary, not far away from a large crypt in the middle of the cemetery.

He and Alia were holding back outside the main gate, but if they didn't go inside soon they would begin to look more and more suspicious—never a good idea when you were by the graves of people's loved ones. Grief made people cranky and made them think you might be up to no good.

"Yeah, we can be nearby in the cemetery. Might give me a chance to find something else to help us."

"Are you actually thinking of grave robbing?" Rich asked.

Alia shrugged and led the way, glancing at his phone now and then to check if she was going in the right direction still or if Natalie had moved.

They caught up with Natalie and Lucas outside the entrance to an old building. This didn't look like a crypt, but like a place of worship that the grieving came to for their burial ceremonies. It was huge.

Rich stood back and stared in awe at what people had created in a time when building big things was difficult and admired that it was still standing. One of the most impressive differences between the US and everything he'd seen in Paris was how old everything was here. Almost everything was older than all the buildings in his own country.

"Any idea what he's doing in there?" Alia asked. She looked the least impressed of all of them to be there.

"We haven't gotten any closer. Figured we should wait until we had all of us as there's three exits from this building. If we're not careful he could decide to walk out of one and we'd never notice." Natalie had a floor plan of the cathedral on her phone screen and pointed out the doors as she spoke.

Rich volunteered to cover one, Alia another, and Natalie took the last one. Lucas couldn't help much with this. Although he could follow a scent and had helped them find the trail of Francisco, it was as if it had taken its toll on the cat holding his human side together and he'd done all the leading that he was going to for the next little while.

Rich picked him up again. It was time to find out what this werewolf was up to.

CHAPTER SEVENTEEN

Glad to have Rich back with them and no longer needing to be a guiding compass for him, Natalie put her phone back in her pocket. It was strange to walk along and follow a cat without making it look as if you were following anyone.

She feared that Francisco had noticed her at least once. The first time, she'd tried to look as if she hadn't been paying him any attention, and looked over a shop display as if it were suddenly the most fascinating thing known to man, but their eyes had met briefly the second time.

That time she'd smiled, trying to be normal and do what she thought a single woman would do if she made eye contact with a hot guy. If nothing else, it might make him overlook her, especially when he was already flirting with a lot of other women and might see her as just another who was momentarily taken in by his charm.

In the back of her mind, she heard Alia telling her not to succumb to something like that. She couldn't live in fear, though. He might charm her, but if she kept her head, she could resist. Could he be any worse than the snakes and con artists that had circled her parents?

Now they were outside a large cathedral, and they knew he was inside but not where. It felt a little like one of those criminal operations where police surrounded a building and then moved in once they had confidence they'd catch the criminals.

There was one big exception. They had only three people and a cat. It wasn't a lot of backup.

They could have called the enforcers and asked them to show up, but Alia didn't want to do that until they knew they could catch the guy and they could make sure they got the evidence. It made Natalie a little uncomfortable, but it wasn't the first time they had defied enforcers to deal with a criminal themselves.

It was a worrying pattern in their lives lately. If nothing else, it wasn't dull, she supposed.

After waiting for Rich and Alia to check in and say they were over their exits, the three of them started stalking forward. For a few seconds, Natalie could see Alia as she moved toward the large front door. Natalie had one of the smaller side doors and Rich had the matching door on the other side.

They rushed until they were close to the doors and hard to see from the windows, and then Natalie crouched to take several deep breaths to calm her heart rate down again. It was only so effective, knowing a dangerous werewolf waited on the other side of the door.

As she inched the door open she got a message from Alia.

No way that I can go in this way without being seen. He's looking this way and there's a direct line of sight to a wide open door.

Natalie frowned and told her to hang back. At least she'd also notice if Francisco tried to flee that way and have a chance of stopping him. Another message from Rich came a few seconds later.

My door is stuck and has some funky hinges. If I open this, he's going to hear it.

That left one thing to do. Natalie had to go in and see if she could get a better look at what Francisco was doing. She opened a video feed for her friends and turned the sound off so they'd be able to hear and see everything she could but nothing would give her away.

She moved forward and passed a small vestibule. The door on the other side stood open and showed the side of the main section of the cathedral. Rows and rows of wooden pews gleamed from the polish and the light coming in from the many windows.

The inside of church buildings had always filled Natalie with awe. So much love went into every detail and she appreciated the effort that went into a congregation singing sounding good. The building itself was designed to be the sweetest sounding, most beautiful place. Whether she agreed with the religion or not, the passion that the makers put in was inspiring.

She stayed crouched as she moved closer, hoping she was quiet enough. She could just barely hear herself moving across the ground, and she had to hope that the werewolf's hearing wasn't much better than a human's.

As she moved into the main body of the cathedral, she paused to figure out where he might be. The pews shielded her as much as they did him from her position. It was the scariest thing she thought she'd ever done and her hands shook as she tried to film and get a better view.

After working her way around to the side, she was able to get into a position where she could see down one of the pews to Francisco and what he was doing. The werewolf was sitting on the floor with several objects laid out in front of him. Natalie couldn't see them well herself, but she used her phone to zoom in and get a better idea.

She was able to make out a strange necklace and several garments, and Natalie recognized some of them from the photos as well as what he had been wearing the last few days. Beside that was a small stack of vials filled with what appeared to be water.

Furthest away from Francisco was an incense burner and several lit candles. It was almost as if he was performing an occult ritual or a religious ceremony. But she had no idea what it was for, or why.

As she saw him pick up the necklace, she shifted to get a better position, lifting herself up to get a better angle. It exposed her a bit more, but he was engrossed and she thought he was unlikely to look her way as long as she didn't make any noise.

She jumped and almost dropped her phone when a hand brushed her back. Turning, she saw Alia, the elf coming up beside her.

"You scared me half to death," she whispered, so quietly

she wasn't sure that Alia had even heard her. The elf was already watching Francisco intently.

"Sorry. I wanted to see what he was up to." She leaned in closer so she could be even quieter.

"What *is* he up to?" Natalie asked.

"Looks like a magic ritual that helps a person hide in plain sight. It would explain why people seem to not be able to recognize him and I've struggled to spot him until he's pointed out. Doesn't work on everyone all the time, but it works enough."

"With water?" Natalie asked, focusing the video in as Francisco took one of the vials and tipped it over the necklace.

"Yeah, you'd be surprised what holy water is good for."

"That's *holy* water? It actually has magical powers?"

Alia nodded.

"Surely it would hurt him though?"

"No. It doesn't do everything you'd think, and werewolves aren't undead. They don't get hurt by holy water. They're just like the other races like elves, dwarves, and humans. They have good and bad among them. Vampires and liches, on the other hand... Those things don't like holy water. If we get a chance we should take a few vials. If they've got some genuine good stuff here, then it's worth having a few bottles."

Natalie blinked. She wasn't sure about the long-term ramifications of stealing from God, but she was also still trying to process the order of beings in the magical realm and what did and didn't work.

Every time Alia talked about anything in her world it gave Natalie and Rich a lot of questions, but the elf had already shown that she didn't always want to answer those questions. She was sometimes a lot more guarded, and Natalie knew enough about her life to know there might be some good reasons. Something bothered her about this werewolf though. Or werewolves in general.

Already they had deviated from the plan so many times that Natalie was starting to wonder if this was personal, but now was not the time to ask.

They held back and watched as Francisco treated the entire pile of clothes and put them all to the side to dry.

"We should call in the enforcers," Natalie whispered when he was almost done.

"Not yet. We still don't know what he's here for. Think of this as part of his getaway plan. It won't work on us because we've seen him prepare it, but it would now work on any backup we called in."

"So you're saying it's too late?"

"It is today. But this wears off."

Natalie tensed her fist and jaw, wishing she'd known sooner. They should have called in enforcers already and handed Francisco over. Instead, they were wasting time and not making any progress.

"We've got the video you're making, and we should be able to find out what artifact he's after, or at least what area of this place it might be buried. Trust me," Alia whispered a moment later.

Their eyes met for a moment as Natalie tried to decide whether she should say something or not. In the end, she nodded. They were too close to danger to ruffle feathers and cause a fuss now.

They looked back to Francisco and focused on the

video again, but saw he was gone. He'd gathered up every-thing and left the empty vials of holy water and candles right there on the floor.

Terrified that he might have noticed them and was ready to strike at any moment, Natalie looked around. She couldn't see him anywhere.

Alia rose until she was standing. She shook her head and strode toward the center of the building and the pile of abandoned ritual items. After blowing out the candles and stoppering the incense, she grabbed the two bottles of holy water that Francisco hadn't used and shoved them into her pocket.

Natalie rolled her eyes and joined the elf more cautiously, still trying to work out where the werewolf had gone. She couldn't see him anywhere and didn't know where to even begin looking. Was this what Alia had meant about him being able to disguise himself? Did that include inside a building like this?

She voiced her fears out loud but Alia shook her head.

"No. It won't work on us, remember. We saw him creating the spell."

As soon as she finished speaking Lucas and Rich came in, both of them coming running through the large, open front door.

"He didn't come out the door by me or this one," Rich insisted. "I don't know where he went, either."

Lucas already had his head near the ground, sniffing around where Francisco had been sitting. Within seconds he was running toward the front of the cathedral, and away from all the exits.

Natalie raised her eyebrows, considering that Francisco

might still be in the building with them. It was a scary thought.

Alia and Rich must have had similar ideas, because they came closer to her and the three of them moved as one, looking for threats to the group and following Lucas.

"There's another exit through this passage somewhere," Lucas reported as they caught up with him by a door and some stairs going downward at the end of the cathedral.

It was tucked behind the choir stands and out of the way, and Natalie didn't like the look of it.

Rich picked up on Natalie's hesitation. "We've got to follow," he told her. "Or we lose our only good lead again."

Natalie grimaced but nodded anyway. Her friends were right, but that didn't mean she had to like going down the creepy passage into something underneath a cathedral in the middle of a cemetery.

CHAPTER EIGHTEEN

Their tabby cat led the way, following a trail. Alia was right behind him, then Natalie, and Rich brought up the rear, using his cell phone as a flashlight.

With her elven eyesight and her comfort being in strange places from all the stuff she'd stolen in the past, Alia didn't need the light, but it helped Natalie and Rich.

Somewhere ahead of them was a werewolf who was clearly up to something and that was never a good thing. Especially when this place was full of magic.

Although she hadn't been able to feel it much in the cathedral, down here in the crypts underneath the large structure, she felt the tug of magic and knew that her thoughts earlier about him coming here for something magical were sound. The place was old enough that all sorts of artifacts were in the place.

If she'd been alone and had time, she would have explored to see if she could find anything worth taking and selling somewhere, but there wasn't time for that. She'd given her word to save the cat in front of her and she was beginning to appreciate her new friends. They made better colleagues than she'd had in the past.

The passage was narrow, and Alia scraped her elbows a couple of times, making more noise each time than she wanted to. It reminded her that she was out of practice. Even more scuffing came from the back of their group, and Rich didn't seem to be doing anything to be careful. It almost didn't matter how much noise she made.

After turning several corners, they came to a small room with many more passages leading away from it. Lucas paused in the middle, sniffing around the floor. Some of the passages seemed to lead to dead ends or obvious tombs of old people with their names carved into stones across the entrance worn with time and fading.

Rich shone his light over a few, reading them while Lucas figured out where to go next. While they were both doing that, Alia was drawn to the pull of something magical much closer. In the corner of the room was a collection of what looked like builders' supplies, repair equipment, a half-full bag of cement powder, and a dust-covered wheelbarrow.

"What is it?" Natalie asked. Alia went over to the pile, drawn in even if she wanted to stop.

"Something magic. I think." Alia let her senses guide her to pull back the top of the cement sack cloth and reveal a small box underneath it. She lifted the wooden container. The whole thing was no bigger than a football, and she felt for the catch holding it shut.

Natalie came to her side as the elf opened it to reveal a small stone with a hand strap attached to it.

"What is that?"

Alia pulled it from the box and slipped it into her hand so the smooth, cold stone was held against her palm. At first, it didn't seem to respond, but she knew it could take a moment for magical items to connect with the mind and power of a new magic user. Anything that was used by one person for a while became attuned to them and harder for others to simply pick up and activate.

She lifted it, knowing it was likely to be aimable, and reached out toward the wall as she gently activated it. Her palm warmed, letting her know it was starting to respond, and then she could feel the stone wall in front of her.

She carefully manipulated a tiny corner to verify that the device did what she was expecting and then she let go again and slipped it off her hand.

She noticed the look on Natalie's face. The young woman stared, open-mouthed and not sure what to make of Alia's magic.

"It's a builders' tool. Of sorts. Might help us."

Rich chuckled as Alia slipped it into a pocket in the depths of her coat and grinned.

"Is it stealing if no one wants it anyway?" she asked when they all looked at her.

Natalie shrugged. "Maybe. But it did look like it had been under there for months."

Lucas flicked his tail back and forth as he padded over to one of the passageways.

"This way," he reported. "I can't smell Francisco down any of the routes, but the way out is this way and there's a breeze that is probably blowing any scent away anyway."

It was logic as good as any and got them all moving again. She didn't want any more focus on what she'd taken or why, so Alia was swift to follow and let Lucas lead the way.

Fearing they had lost even more time on the werewolf as he went on with his mission, they jogged along until they came toward another section that opened up again.

A grave of sorts, with someone inside a stone box ornately carved in the middle of a stone structure, lay in front of steps leading up to a door on the other side.

A small section of evening light came through a gap in the door, showing that it hadn't been shut properly by the last person who had used it. Lucas darted around the centerpiece and carried on toward the door.

Happy to be back outside and sure she wasn't alone in that sentiment, Alia followed the cat. She reached for the new magical device, but Rich stayed her hand.

"Let's not make it too obvious we're here. And if it might run out, definitely don't waste it."

He had a point, but she wanted to use it anyway. Since the enforcers had taken away the majority of her magical objects, she had missed how much easier they made some things. It was addictive to be able to do something a normal person couldn't, to make life easier and save time and effort.

It wasn't sensible, though, and Rich was right. Magical items could run out of power, and she didn't know what was left in this stone. It might have been left practically forgotten because it didn't have much strength left in it. That was the trouble with stealing your magical possessions. You never knew if they were any good or not until too late.

Lucas didn't have to pick up on Francisco's scent again,

because Natalie spotted the werewolf in the far distance. They were all silent, none of them wanting to draw attention to themselves while they followed.

Francisco didn't rush but strolled along casually. The werewolf was tall, however, and that meant Alia was practically jogging to keep up.

Across the vast cemetery, there wasn't a lot of cover, but there were enough headstones, crypt entrances, and statues that they could follow him without always having a direct line of sight. It was also growing darker. The sun had almost set in the time they'd been in the cathedral.

Francisco stopped now and then, giving them a chance to catch up, but Rich also stopped a couple of times and held them back.

"We can't just keep following this guy around," Rich insisted when the werewolf stopped by another crypt. "We need to get this guy arrested. It's clear that he's here looking for something magical."

"I want the evidence he's taken."

"So let's trap him somewhere, call for the enforcers and we can get the evidence out of him while we're waiting for them to show up. They're not going to get here immediately."

Alia exhaled and tried not to show her initial reaction to the words. Rich was right, but she didn't want him to be. She couldn't work out what she did want, though. Not entirely. What was it about this werewolf that made her want to hunt him down?

"Okay. When he's inside a crypt and trying to get something." She nodded and pulled the stone she'd taken back out again and slipped it onto her hand.

It was all the confirmation they needed. As Francisco approached yet another crypt and checked it out, the three of them fanned out a little to surround it if he went inside.

"We look a little like the Scooby gang." Natalie smirked as she looked between the four of them.

"In those old cartoons? With the dog and the painted van?" Alia asked.

"I think Natalie means in Buffy. The group of kids that helped Buffy patrol the city at night to defend against vampires and stuff."

"Oh. I never saw that show."

"You didn't?" Natalie almost tripped over a grave as she looked at Alia instead of where she was going.

"Nope. It was hokey and nothing like us in real life. Why would any of us magical folks watch something like that?"

"Good point."

"We're cooler," Lucas added as he jumped up onto the plinth of a large memorial statue.

Alia grinned as Francisco moved to the next crypt. When they reached the one he'd been at a minute or so earlier, she paused. A faint pull of magical energy came from inside this one as well, and it tugged at Alia's mind. She was tempted to let the others go ahead and see what this one contained.

She resisted the urge to steal more from the dead and continued with the group after the werewolf. He seemed to have taken more of an interest in the next crypt, not just shifting the opening and looking in this time, but stepping inside.

Taking the opportunity, they rushed up and

surrounded the crypt. At the same time, Alia activated the device she held to manipulate the stone, closing the entrance to the crypt and trying to set it so even a werewolf of his strength couldn't open it.

"Ah, I wondered if you three were just curious or had intentions," an enigmatic voice called from inside the tomb.

"Game's up, Francisco," Alia informed him. She felt something resist her magic a little, the stone pushing back against her control and the device. It heated up a little more in her palm but it was still cool enough that she could hold it without burning.

"Well, you certainly have some power, little elf, but you're not going to have this easy. Nothing personal. I just don't like small spaces."

Rich grinned at the goofy quip and Alia could have smacked him. Why did a werewolf like Francisco have to be so good at the charm spell?

This wasn't going to be an easy battle.

CHAPTER NINETEEN

The crypt seemed to warp and shift before Rich's eyes as Alia and Francisco fought for control of the door. Rich shook his head a couple of times, trying to clear it of the desire to stop Alia and he had to forcibly keep his mouth shut to not call out anything to the werewolf inside.

After talking to Francisco for so long at the bar, he wanted to ask him for another story, or to tell one of them again. Just to listen to him talk. Instead, he watched his friend try to trap the werewolf inside a crypt.

Lucas sat near him and watched.

"Not much we can do while they fight," the cat pointed out when Rich tried to encourage him to help in some way.

"Actually there is something you can do," Alia called back, having heard them.

A moment later she took a couple of steps their way and aimed the funky stone she had at a different section of the crypt.

"He's trying to break out of various places and I need you to spot where."

Lucas bounded up onto the structure, careful to avoid the area Alia was currently battling over. It bulged out toward them for a few seconds before she forced it back in.

"Can you keep this up?" Natalie asked as Francisco made another area weaken.

"I don't know, but I'm going to try."

"You are a determined one, *ma chère*," Francisco called from inside, breaking through enough to be able to hear them clearly.

"And you don't know when you've lost," Alia snapped back.

Rich wanted to ask for a truce, something that could let them discuss this like normal people, not sure he understood the anger, but as he went to get in Alia's way to suggest just that, Lucas jumped off the crypt top and yowled at him.

"What the hell, Lucas?" he exclaimed and tried to push the rogue cat away.

"Focus on the task," Lucas shot back, encouraging Rich to back up so Alia could come flying around to yet another forming hole. This time, Francisco managed to get a gap wide enough that they could see his head. Natalie threw a rock at him, making him duck back inside and lose his concentration.

"Good aim, *ma chère*. You can throw well for a human. I have underestimated your talents in this field while I was distracted by your beauty."

"You're not charming another one of my… colleagues," Alia yelled. She closed the gap once more.

Sweat was beading on her forehead as they all spread out.

"I'm not charmed," Rich insisted as he stumbled over a headstone and tried to focus on helping.

"Yes, you are. You're practically useless in this fight," Natalie replied as she went the other way and Lucas went over the top again. "Over here," she called to Alia.

Natalie picked up another rock as Alia came around again. They were fighting back and forth but no one was getting anywhere long term and all it was doing was draining two magical artifacts and wearing everyone out.

For a few more seconds, Rich watched, wondering if something else could be done, but Francisco was soon trying to get out where he was.

Intent on proving that he was on the side of his friends and had a mind of his own, he stooped to pick up a rock as well. It felt heavy in his hand as Alia came around to tackle yet another opening.

Francisco's head reappeared and he flicked a wink at Rich. Still Rich stood there.

"Help!" Alia shouted at him as she stopped at his side and focused the device on the hole.

Almost in slow motion, Rich flung the rock. It was on target enough that it hit the edge of the hole and ricocheted off and inside. Of course, it missed Francisco. For some reason, Rich couldn't bring himself to hit the werewolf, which was far worse than anything any of them could have said to show him he was charmed.

"Poor shot," the werewolf ribbed as Alia fought to close the hole and Natalie threw a much better-aimed rock that forced him to pull back. "I'd say you throw like a girl, but this dark-haired beauty is putting many a man to shame with her fierce display."

"Shut up," Alia yelled. Rich thought the elf was trying to make sure none of the others were charmed as well.

Before Francisco could retort, the stone closed over the gap with a snap and he was shut off from them again for a moment.

"We really should call the enforcers," Natalie fretted, but Rich couldn't bring himself to do that either and Alia clearly wasn't going to get the chance.

Lucas jumped as Francisco shifted the stone under him. Although Rich couldn't do much else to help, he gave Alia a boost up onto the top. He noticed she was panting and seemed tired but she was determined to keep going and ensure Francisco didn't get out.

It wasn't the first time he had noticed that Alia seemed to have a problem with either this werewolf or werewolves in general. What he didn't understand was *why*. She hadn't struck him as the sort of person to hold a grudge against an entire race. And she was a thief and a bit of a rogue at times. Surely she couldn't have a problem with Francisco being a conman? Yes, he'd stolen evidence, but they had no idea why.

Rich shook his head, his gaze on Alia as she fought on top of the crypt, each foot seeking solid stone as Francisco kept changing patches to destabilize her. He barely dared to breathe as she seemed to dance back and forth. He both feared for her safety and wanted Francisco to make it out.

Being charmed sucked. He wanted to help his friends and it was as if his brain was stuck, thinking of hurting them or hindering them or just being useless.

It was infuriating and he was getting a little sick of it.

But he had no idea how to make his body do something if his mind didn't want to.

Francisco gave up on trying to get out of the roof, but he almost got Alia stuck when her leg went through a hole as she tried to get down again.

For a few seconds, the tables turned and the werewolf was trying to close the stone around her leg while she tried to keep it free and Natalie threw stones and Lucas tried to swipe through gaps.

Rich selected a carefully considered stone. Something smooth and flat, rounded. The kind of stone you would select on a pebble beach or by a lake to skim. This time he took a deep breath, focused on wanting to hurl the rock at the werewolf and that this was the right thing to do to help his friends.

He threw it as hard as he could.

This time it did fly through the gap, and Francisco had to duck to not get hit by it. It hit something behind him with a loud crack and enough force to damage it.

"Now that is more like it, Rich! You are no longer so smitten you think me unhittable. But the dark-haired beauty still defeats you in fierceness. She is one with her passions and uses them like a driving force."

"And you'll be one with a crypt in another few minutes if you don't give in and let us hand you over to the authorities. The enforcers are after you and there's no running and hiding from us. We can find you, no matter what you're wearing and where you go." Alia got her foot free and started to close the gap again.

Francisco appeared to be amused at the antics more than anything else, grinning as he fought his way out of the crypt. The original structure was unrecognizable. It was distorted and morphed and any carvings that had been there were now gone. Rich felt a little bad but there wasn't anything he could do. He couldn't use magic and even if he could, he doubted he would be able to restore works of art.

"I can't keep doing this." Alia's words were quiet and muffled so the werewolf wouldn't be able to hear her.

Almost as soon as she finished speaking, the werewolf burst through another section again. Natalie screamed and let the creature through. Alia couldn't get around to that side of the crypt fast enough, and the device in her hands sparked. She yelped and dropped it.

"It broke?" Natalie recovered and pelted Francisco with another stone.

"No. Overheated of sorts. Needed a break." Alia tried to pick it up again, but it fizzled some more and made her wince, so she didn't try to put it on again.

"A little help over here," Lucas called before hissing and lashing out at the werewolf as he wriggled through the gap.

They could do nothing as he squeezed out of the gap he'd made. Their only solace was that he had also worn out the device that controlled the stone from his side, and he threw it on the ground by the crypt as he struggled out.

Natalie risked getting close to the dangerous foe to grab his device as he found his feet and tried to run off. The burly creature almost flung Lucas to one side, and the cat yowled.

Seeing all his friends in danger seemed to snap Rich out of his funk. He sprinted after the werewolf, hurling another rock at the same time.

Their only option was to give chase. Alia and Natalie

soon caught up and Lucas bounded even faster ahead to recover some of the gap.

The werewolf ran off down the rows of graves toward the exit and the city beyond. If they didn't do something about it, he was going to get out, but Rich had no idea what could be done. This entire plan had been half-baked from the beginning, and he'd been too charmed to call the enforcers when he'd had the chance.

He hoped that, with the amount of magic they had been throwing around, now there would be something the magic police could pick up on that would bring the law down on their side. The big question was whether they would show up in time or not.

Francisco was still fifty yards or so from the cemetery gates when Alia and Natalie's magical devices cooled enough to stop being temperamental. Alia instructed Natalie on what to do while they ran, lagging behind a little so Natalie could figure it out.

Nothing happened for Natalie at first, but then a chunk of gravestone flew up and toward Francisco.

"I did it," Natalie squealed.

"And magic, even if a little…crude, *ma chère*," Francisco called. "We are really proving our mettle today, no?"

"And she's not being charmed by you either," Alia yelled. She had switched her focus to the gates ahead and was melding and morphing the stone on either side of them to close the gap.

It was an impressive feat, and even Francisco realized that he wasn't going to make it before Alia had closed it off, not while Natalie was also flinging bits of stone at him.

Rich continued to hurl whatever he could put his hands on, though he frequently missed as well.

Francisco opted for an unexpected course and ran to a nearby tree. Before any of them could react, he swung himself up into the branches and climbed in a way no human could have managed.

They gathered around the bottom. Lucas didn't dare follow without them, and the werewolf was already barely visible among the foliage. He was high enough and surrounded by enough branches that they had no clear shot at him with anything.

"You can't stay up there forever," Lucas yelled before he jumped at the tree trunk to climb up.

Higher up, the tree went still. "Is that a cursed human? In cat form?"

CHAPTER TWENTY

"Strange. He looks very much like a cat, but he's definitely talking like a human, yes?" Francisco pressed.

Natalie frowned, not sure what to make of this creature. He taunted and flattered them, and she could feel a pull in her mind trying to tell her to like him, but at the same time, she wanted to stab him with something sharp to stop him from mocking them or charming Rich any further. It appeared as if her friend might have recovered, though.

"He's cursed," Natalie confirmed.

"Interesting. And beginning to lose himself? Not a recent curse. One you can't break. I could perhaps negotiate a curse breaking for you? I know many people across the world. Have someone persuade the caster to lift it."

"The elf who cast it is dead," Alia shot back, the anger in her voice clear. They were all sick of explaining what would inevitably follow.

"Interesting. A curse not broken on death. This must be very frustrating for you all, no?"

Natalie looked at Alia and Rich and then they all looked at Lucas. The cat had paused at the bottom of the tree. The werewolf had their attention for a moment.

Natalie tried to figure out how to get the strange stone nestled against her palm to work again. It hadn't been easy the first time, and she had sucked at any level of control. Thankfully it didn't seem to need much to get it to fling bits of stone and rock at force. It had turned off in the time Francisco had already been in the tree, but she didn't know how to turn it on again.

"I know an artifact that might cure him," the werewolf offered. Lucas hopped down and circled the tree, trying to get a better view of Francisco.

"You're just saying that," Alia yelled back.

"I never 'just say' anything. Words are important and not to be wasted. I can help you get your friend back before it's too late to save him. The artifact I seek and the one you need are in the same place."

Natalie started to relax, but Alia stepped forward to glare up into the tree branches. She aimed her stone as if she could morph the tree with it. It didn't appear to be working and Alia looked even more angry.

"If you just let me come down—"

"Absolutely not," Alia interrupted. "We don't trust you. You're under arrest."

Natalie thought she heard a growl come from above.

"You have made a deal with the enforcers, have you not?" he asked.

"Something like that," Rich replied before clapping his hand over his mouth. Natalie rolled her eyes, but didn't mind too much. It was almost comical seeing Rich so charmed and unable to stop himself from doing things.

Alia glared at him, and Natalie had to stifle her reaction as a chuckle threatened to come out of her. Lucas, however, was flicking his tail back and forth and backing up to clearly take a running jump at the tree.

"Let us see if we can reach an agreement before your furry friend hurts himself trying to get to me, shall we?"

"I'm not making a deal with a werewolf." Alia tried to activate the stone on the tree again, but still nothing happened.

"Surely it is not your deal to decline, elf."

The animosity between Alia and Francisco was definitely a race thing. Natalie wondered what had triggered it, but she didn't feel as if she could ask. If Alia was allowed to have her way, though, it wouldn't necessarily be the right thing for the group as a whole or Lucas, and that meant stepping in.

"What do you have in mind?" Natalie asked. "But spit it out and don't bother if it's a stupid deal. We're not interested in having our time wasted."

"Thank you for listening. I will be brief and assume your knowledge of certain things. If I understand correctly, you have made a deal with the enforcers to turn me in to them or help catch me. A noble but ultimately futile goal. But I know how to help your friend. Because you have made a deal, I am sure that you believe others are watching, especially outside in this situation. Therefore, you must make it look as if you are hunting me."

"We already do look like we're hunting you. You're stuck up a tree and we're standing around the bottom." Alia looked as if she might start hurling gravestones any minute.

Natalie stepped forward again. "Hurry up. What are you proposing?"

"It is simple really. You continue to hunt me but let me keep getting away. I will lead you to the artifact I seek and what you need to cure your friend. Although I confess, he's a very fine specimen of a cat."

"Make one more comment on me being a feline and I'll come up there and…" Lucas ran at the tree again.

He only got part way up the trunk, digging his claws into the bark before he ran out of oomph and had to jump down again. Although Lucas was getting used to being a cat, there were still some things that he couldn't do as well as real cats could.

Rich stepped closer to Natalie and Alia. "We took this job because we thought it might help us save Lucas," he muttered. "If there's a chance that he could lead us to something that might help, I think we have to—"

"You're just charmed by him," Alia snapped.

"I actually think Rich might be right," Natalie added, glancing up to see if Francisco was close enough to hear them talking. "We've been trying to get Lucas back the whole time and I think we need to at least consider this."

"No. We're not making a deal with a werewolf. How do we know that he'll keep his word?"

Rich shrugged. "We don't need to. If he doesn't, we stop following him as a ruse and call the enforcers down on him properly."

"But we can't. Of course he wants a deal. We have him cornered and he knows it. This is what he does!"

Natalie hesitated. Alia could be right. They had a conman up a tree, and he was trying to talk his way down. But they had to save Lucas and they couldn't do so without some help. They had already exhausted every avenue they could think of.

She would never forgive herself if Lucas was stuck as a cat for the rest of his life and they later found out they could have cured him if they'd taken a risk.

"Okay," Natalie called up. "What do you have in mind to convince the enforcers?"

"Find me tomorrow at the clock tower and I'll lead you there." Francisco sounded smug.

Alia stuck to her guns. "We're not taking our eyes off you. You're taking us there now."

"I cannot. It's simply not possible. The artifact I seek and therefore the one you want is not here and that means I have got a vital piece of information wrong. Thankfully, there is only one other place both can be. We're lucky that I know this place as well and can help us both benefit from its riches."

"I don't like this," Alia muttered under her breath, but Natalie shrugged.

They had nothing to lose and everything to gain.

"You better be there," Natalie replied. "You know that we can find you if we need to. We've found you three days in a row, and we've got you cornered now. We can do it again."

"Noted, but even if that were not the case, I might be a conman, but when I give someone my word, they have my word." Francisco peered out of the foliage, no longer trying to hide.

Alia went to use the device on her hand to hurl a chunk of gravestone at him, but Natalie stopped her and encouraged everyone to take a step back.

Despite them backing off, Francisco wouldn't come down the tree until Alia had reopened the gates and at least attempted to put the stone back where it ought to be before taking the magic stone off her hand again.

Natalie tried to hand the elf the second stone, but Alia shook her head.

"No. You keep it. I can't wield more than one and who knows when we might benefit from both of us using something like that. You can practice with it if you want."

"I can't even get it turned on again," Natalie complained. While she had been trying to stop Francisco, she hadn't been thinking about what she'd been doing, but now that she had a moment, she wasn't sure it was something she wanted to be involved in.

After a moment of hesitation, she shoved the stone deep into her bag and opted to forget about it for now. She had bigger things to worry about, like helping Lucas and figuring out what Francisco's angle was.

Francisco climbed down, and after giving them a brief bow, he fled. Natalie watched him go. The sky was much darker than when their chase had begun.

A nagging thought wouldn't leave her alone: this wasn't likely to be a smooth journey. Something always went wrong.

CHAPTER TWENTY-ONE

There were so many mixed feelings inside Alia that she didn't know what to say to her companions the whole time they were heading back to their apartment in Paris.

Even when they stopped off briefly to get supplies for dinner and were trying to discuss what to make, she felt uninterested. And dinner was something that usually caught her interest. It was so lovely having access to money and ingredients and not having to eat yet another packet of ramen or cheap snacks.

On top of that, the fresh fruit and vegetables seemed to be cheaper here and more abundant. It was something that had excited her at first, but today it held no appeal.

When they stepped into the space they were renting, Alia was feeling even worse. She'd let the others overrule her because she knew how much Lucas meant to them and it had become clear that they were so set on trying to save him that nothing she could have said would have stopped them.

She didn't blame them. She was pissed off and wanted

to recover all the evidence Francisco had and see him behind bars, but they were trying to save a friend.

She didn't trust him, though.

"You have a face like thunder and haven't said a word beyond 'okay' and 'sure' since we left the cemetery," Natalie pointed out to Alia as they all sat to eat the pasta dish Rich had prepared for them.

"You don't like us letting Francisco go, do you?" Rich added as he put a smaller bowl in front of Lucas. It had all been chopped up into small enough chunks, and seeing that almost made Alia say nothing.

"I don't like it," she replied anyway. She couldn't help but say what was on her mind.

They waited. No one interrupted her and no one blew up. For a moment, she couldn't speak. She hadn't expected them to be so calm in the face of her expressing a differing opinion.

"I don't trust him, and I really don't think he was telling the truth. A werewolf can't be trusted to do anything but lie and cheat and do whatever they think is best to get what they want. They don't care about anyone who isn't in their pack. Everyone in the magical world knows that about werewolves. And Francisco doesn't have a pack."

"Am I right in thinking that elves don't get along very well with weres and don't like them very much?" Natalie asked.

"We don't. At all and for very good reasons. They cannot be trusted. Francisco especially."

"Are there stories and things that are passed around in the elven world, then?" Rich probed gently. "Like, are there examples of things?"

Alia frowned. It was common knowledge.

"Probably. It's something we all know. We do our best to get along with them, but we don't trust them and we definitely don't go into business with them."

"But has one ever betrayed you personally? How common is it for elves to interact with werewolves. Are there any positive experiences?" Natalie continued eating when she finished asking her questions, but Alia frowned.

"It's just something we all know, okay. I can't explain it. It's the way things are in the magical community. We do what we have to do to keep ourselves safe. A lot of elves don't have it as easy as you think. And I know we shouldn't trust Francisco. He's done some really shady things, and there's all that evidence. So many victims aren't getting justice."

Rich frowned and looked at Natalie and Lucas.

"Natalie was right about one thing. We'll track him down again. He's not leaving the area, and the enforcers have put us on the task. So we haven't let him go without having a way to make sure we catch him again."

"Yeah, I'm not worried about that either. He's looking for something and is working from here. We'll find him again no matter where he goes." Alia sat back, still eating but wanting to make sure that she was getting her thoughts across right.

"So it bothers you more that we're trusting him than we let him go?" Rich asked.

"Yes."

Natalie put her fork down. "I don't know if we can trust him either. And I won't pretend to even understand exactly what happened between elves and werewolves or where your distrust comes from. I'm not going to judge it. But I do know that if we don't take the chance to help Lucas and we lose him, I wouldn't be okay with it for as long as I lived."

The passion in Natalie's words hit Alia hard. She gulped and nodded, and Natalie went on. "So how about when we get what we want, we double cross *him*."

Alia blinked, not sure she was hearing right. Was Natalie suggesting that they become traitors themselves?

"If he's as bad as we think, and he really has stolen all that evidence, then we can just hand him over once Lucas is human again. We only have to work with him long enough to get our friend back."

"You'd really all be okay with that?" Alia couldn't quite believe Natalie's words, though she knew the woman was straight talking and reliable.

"This werewolf is definitely a criminal. He's confessed as much. All we're doing is getting what we need before we do what we've always been planning. Handing him over to the authorities and making sure that he can't get out again."

"And we never told him that we wouldn't," Rich added. "He asked us to let him down from the tree in return for helping us fix Lucas. Technically, we've done that."

"And he sort of implied that we needed to not help the enforcers until he'd got whatever artifact he's also after." Natalie went back to eating as Alia felt herself relaxing again. Her two friends were listening to her, and they were going to help her catch a criminal after all. Sometimes she needed to remind herself that people could be trusted to do the right thing. You just had to give them a chance.

It was a sort-of plan, and having it made her feel calmer.

They were delaying his capture and the return of the evidence, but that was a lot better than letting him go outright. Now all she had to do was make sure to stay a step ahead of him. They had to make sure he didn't con them as he had others in the past. And that meant Alia had to look out for any sign of treachery and protect her human friends.

CHAPTER TWENTY-TWO

As Rich finished breakfast, eating it on the way to the clock tower Francisco had suggested, he felt more than a little trepidation, though he'd never have mentioned it to the others.

He'd felt similar when they had gone to confront Daven and try to free Lucas. They were on the same quest still, but this was different. Francisco was more of an unknown. Alia had been sure of their course of action the last time.

It seemed with every day they had in the magical world, they got themselves deeper, but he didn't mind. He'd never felt more alive.

They continued through more of Paris, with Lucas riding on Rich's shoulder. The city was beginning to lose its romantic charm as he discovered more of the magic and the way some unfortunate members of the magic community lived. The world needed help, and a lot of injustice needed addressing.

Magic seemed to make it easier for those with power to oppress those without.

The clock tower in question came into view. Some tourists already milled around, but Rich saw no sign of the werewolf yet. Of course, every other time they had been looking for him, it had been the glasses or Lucas who had found Francisco, and Rich had no reason to believe that this would be any different.

It was strange to see so many people going about their day. He thought about how much more of the world he knew of than most of them now. A werewolf was nearby and most of these people had no clue that they even existed, let alone that a dangerous one was in their midst.

"This is stupid. It's early and busy and I can't believe that we're even doing this. How can we seriously be considering trusting and meeting this guy?" Alia folded her arms across her chest and looked as if she wanted to hit something or someone. Rich understood her reluctance, but they needed to give things a chance.

"He's here," Natalie reported less than three seconds later, grinning and glancing at Alia as she did. Wearing their glasses, Natalie was the one who could see their quarry more easily. Lucas could smell him, but only if they got close enough.

For a few minutes, Francisco wandered, appearing to deliberately dither, but staying busy in that area browsing wares in stalls and buying street food from a vendor.

While the werewolf ate his breakfast, they could get closer to him and try to work out what he was up to and where he planned to go.

They were still a couple of hundred yards away when Francisco spotted them, grinned briefly before eating the last bite of a croissant, and turned to head into the crowds.

Rich followed and tried not to think about where the werewolf could be leading them. This could be some wild goose chase, but for their friend's sake, he hoped not.

Lucas was surprisingly silent, resting on Rich's shoulders while Natalie and Alia went ahead of him. Since those two were keeping an eye on their quarry, Rich looked around a bit more and tried to take in where they were going and what to expect from the area. Not all parts of a city were created equal.

Despite their fears, the werewolf didn't appear to be doing anything that would help him get away from them too much. He was just staying a certain distance away from them.

It was tiring and his shoulders soon ached from carrying Lucas, but in a city like Paris, with so many tourists and busy streets, it was safer to have the cat on his shoulders.

Francisco led them through some of the busiest areas of Paris and seemed to be going in circles at first, but they followed and Natalie kept her eyes fixed on him the entire time. Now that she'd gotten used to being in the city and the glasses had more of the data for the people and places stored in its memory banks, she'd reported that there was less lag and less overwhelm. She was also careful not to look right at large groups or crowds of people.

It made her appear to be a little strange, but she was keeping them on Francisco's track. Alia made sure Natalie didn't walk into the path of a car or bump into people by linking arms and steering her. After half an hour of doing this the pair were practiced at it.

After a long day following Francisco around Paris, Rich was thrilled when the werewolf finally felt it was safe to approach them and suggested an early dinner. It had felt very natural being with Francisco at the bar the first night Rich had met him, and sitting down to eat with him and Rich's other friends felt no different. Alia was quiet and didn't say much, appearing to prefer to tuck into the food and try to eat her weight in shrimp and fresh bread.

Natalie seemed to have the opposite idea, hanging on Francisco's every word as he talked about some of the different meals he had eaten in different places. She barely touched a bite herself while Rich fed Lucas.

Although the cat had been able to stomach a lot of human food at first, Rich had noticed his diet becoming more limited as time went on, and had made it one of his duties to help Lucas stay healthy. That meant a good portion of the shrimp and some tuna from a tuna salad had gone down to ground level on another plate.

Everything else, Rich had broken up and given Lucas a little of. Enough to get the taste but not enough to make him puke. No one wanted to clean cat puke, especially since Lucas had begun licking himself to keep clean, like a normal cat.

It was obvious that Francisco appreciated their company and enjoyed having people with him on his travels for once, especially with Natalie mooning at him. Rich would have said she was as charmed as he had been, but he suspected that it might be worse. Alia seemed unconcerned, though.

The werewolf finished eating and put his knife and fork together. "And all good things must come to an end." Natalie seemed to notice half her food still sat on her plate. She blinked a few times, and Rich considered teasing her about being too charmed to eat, but Francisco clocked it as well and Rich didn't want to give the werewolf any more satisfaction.

"I think we'd all best get some sleep." He made sure Francisco was under his gaze so the werewolf would know he was the main recipient of his words. "Especially if you're to guide us to our important artifact tomorrow."

"Yes, I shall leave you all to finish your dinner and retire. I have taken enough of your time. Thank you, Natalie, for listening to an old werewolf reminisce for a while."

"I enjoy hearing about other cultures and learning, but Rich is right, we need you at your best for tomorrow. We want our friend back, and that's the big reason we're here with you."

Rich raised his eyebrows at the coldness and warning in Natalie's words. Was she fighting being charmed, or had she never been in the first place? Either way, it was impressive, and Francisco appeared to respect it. He bowed to her before returning to wherever he was staying.

As soon as he was gone, they all relaxed a little and the conversation picked up again with the pressure off. Four friends, having dinner together and off on an adventure of their own.

CHAPTER TWENTY-THREE

As the sky lightened, Alia frowned. They were meant to be sneaking out of their rooms and to the train station before it was light to reduce the chance that an enforcer saw them. They didn't know for sure that any were nearby—Rich felt fairly confident that he'd dealt with the only ones on their trail—but there was no such thing as being too careful.

For now, they'd split up with Francisco again. Rich was carrying Lucas inside some sort of portmanteau, and they were all carrying their luggage again. Francisco was going to meet them on the platform when they gave him the signal that the coast was clear.

It took all of Alia's encouragement and teaching to get Natalie and Rich to move quietly enough and in the right way to keep moving without drawing the attention of enforcers if they were around.

Natalie had learned fast, as she seemed to with everything else, but anything physical wasn't Rich's strong point.

Her only solace was that he was no longer charmed by the werewolf.

Alia couldn't decide what to make of Francisco anymore. He had been so certain that he was doing the right thing and hadn't done anything evil. That was the way with a lot of very evil people, and they often believed they were right, but something about him was more innocent than she had expected.

He genuinely appeared to care. And so far they had been able to trust him, but Alia had learned the hard way that it was when people were finally beginning to seem as if they were your friend and that they might be on your side that they tended to double cross. If Francisco was going to do anything to betray them it would be soon.

All these thoughts and more went through her head as they wound through streets that were already beginning to grow busier. Being in the country's capital city was an eye opening experience and Alia made the mental note to come back here when she had time to sight-see. It was a beautiful place and Natalie, wearing the glasses again, kept whispering about elements of magic used here and there.

It gave the indication that there was a strong magical community in the city and the designs of a lot of the buildings reminded her of some of the elven places other elves had told her about when she had been growing up. Some of it was interesting to her.

As they got closer to the train station the streets grew busier and the tactics needed to be changed. Instead of trying to move silently, it was time to blend in with the crowd and look as if they were yet another citizen going about their business.

It was something Natalie struggled with more, especially while wearing the glasses and needing to be careful where she looked, but Rich put an arm through hers this time, making it appear as if they were a couple. That left Alia to follow along behind and check that they weren't being followed.

In this manner, they could also walk much quicker. They soon got to the train station, and Rich bought the tickets to the destination Francisco had written. And then they made their way to the platform.

On the platform, Alia didn't see the werewolf, not even in a disguise that might pass for him. There simply wasn't anyone tall enough. Knowing the location they were aiming for had made Alia consider double crossing Francisco first and not showing up, or trying to get an earlier train, or going a different route, anything that would get them there under their own steam and without him, but it hadn't occurred to her that he might not show up until now.

Had he given them the wrong location?

Alia frowned and realized they had made a big mistake. She doubted the place they had been given was the right location. Francisco had ditched them. It was so simple that she could have kicked herself.

"I can't see him yet," Natalie confirmed, not even trying to hide her attempts to see him yet.

"We've still got fifteen minutes before the train goes," Rich added, looking at his watch. "And we don't know if he might have run into enforcers. There's a chance he's having to get rid of company of his own."

"We've got to get on that train either way." Natalie

pointed out. "If there's even a chance that it's the right place to go and he'll join us along the way, or we can find that artifact while he rots in a jail cell then we need to take it."

Although she had a point, Alia didn't want to admit it. She wanted to throw something. This was her sort of game, the part of life that she was meant to be good at. Sneaking around and stealing stuff while under the enforcers' noses. Being outplayed got to her.

As each minute ticked by, she grew more and more tense. This was worse than keeping watch for enforcers while someone else burgled a house. At least then she wasn't worried about herself or anyone she cared about as much. But this could screw over Lucas, and she'd begun to like the fur ball.

"There he is." Natalie's voice was a quiet squeak that Alia was sure had meant to come out as a whisper. She rolled her eyes but the relief that swept through her was palpable. Her hands relaxed, leaving behind several half-moons on her palms where her fingernails had dug in.

Rich grinned and gave a little wave to the tall figure Natalie had pointed out. He was wearing a different hat and coat, but he was wheeling familiar luggage along behind him.

With two minutes to spare, he reached them, smiling as if this had always been the plan and he hadn't intended to do anything but cut it this fine.

The train pulled up a few seconds later, and they hurried onto it, Francisco leading the way. This train wasn't going far and didn't have separate compartments, forcing the four of them to find table seats where they could put the portmanteau on the table and open it enough to give Lucas some wriggle room.

It was a tight squeeze, and Francisco was the least comfortable looking of the three of them. Alia was the shortest, and she also made sure that she was near the window. Rich sat opposite her and Natalie beside her.

Alia looked out for enforcers and anyone else getting on the train with them, but this early in the day it was relatively quiet and the train wasn't in the station long enough for anyone to have gotten on with them who hadn't already been on the platform when it had arrived.

"I think we're clear," Alia reported as the train picked up speed and took them out of the station.

"I believe so as well. We have about two hours until we arrive at our destination." Francisco grinned.

"I must admit, I'll be happy to not see another train for a while after this," Rich put in.

"I've traveled a lot the last few years, seeing the world. Trains can get tedious sometimes, but they are one of the best ways to truly see the places you travel through. Especially a local train like this. We'll go through towns and villages, we'll see the countryside, the rich and the poor."

"What's had you traveling so much?" Rich asked. He kept looking between Francisco and the view out of the window, as if he couldn't decide whether to give the werewolf his attention or the view that he'd praised.

Alia stifled her amused grin and went back to staring out the window, determined to drink it all in even if she listened along the way.

"There are many artifacts in this world. Many of them used to be in the hands of the werewolves. My kind doesn't perform magic or have its own reserves to tap into the way other races do. We have to use powerful artifacts and learn to wield them. We have strength and we have speed. We have charm of a sort, but we were once a very respected race which used all these artifacts for the betterment of our kind and all the others we looked out for."

"You're protectors," Natalie suggested.

"Yes. We were. But our artifacts were all taken from us for one reason or another. I have spent the last few years trying to get them back. I've not always gone about this in…perfectly honest ways, but I have only taken what was once ours and then returned it to the correct descendant of the were who held it last."

"And is that what you're looking for today?" Rich asked. "As well as the device to break the curse on Lucas?"

"Yes. And even if you hadn't cornered me up a tree in a cemetery, had I understood the plight of your friend I would have offered to help you find the artifact you needed. It is what our kind does for those who need our aid. I really won't double cross you. All I ask is that I be allowed to look for the artifact I seek as well."

No one spoke after this passionate statement. Alia couldn't be sure if she believed him or not, but she knew that at least part of it was true. Werewolves had once been protectors and held a lot of artifacts, but she had been taught that their own actions changed that. They had destroyed themselves by being too greedy and trying to overpower other races.

Clearly Francisco didn't think this, however. Or, at least

it wasn't what he took pride in or what he said he was trying to restore. He appeared to be honest when he said he wanted to help Lucas, although no matter how much Alia wanted to believe it, she couldn't let her guard down.

Her friends needed her to be on her guard.

CHAPTER TWENTY-FOUR

Strange feelings washed over Natalie as she walked behind Francisco. They had gotten off the train a few minutes earlier, found some safe storage for their luggage, and then he had led them on foot to their destination. The town they were in was beautiful. All old red brick and quaint, but full of life and flowers and people who cared about what little they had.

Francisco had led them down a few busier streets and then up an old dirt track until they came to where they were now: the driveway to an old, dilapidated mansion. It had clearly once stood as one of the more majestic buildings in town, and Natalie didn't doubt that it would have some gorgeous views from the top windows.

It was both splendid and sad, and the werewolf in front of her seemed to take on the same demeanor. His body was striking as he strode up to it, but she saw a sadness in the way he looked over the exterior and took in the lack of care.

A small section of guttering had come loose, and the

driveway had several years of dead leaves that had turned to mulch across it. The flower beds on either side of the lawn had become choked with weeds and brambles, and the lawn was weeds and tall grasses. No one lived here. No one cared about it.

Francisco walked right up to the front door, a large wooden double paneled opening. It had two large handles set in the center and a bell rope on one side. He didn't ring it, but pulled a key from his pocket and used it to open the door.

Had he been carrying the key to this place all along? Was this his house? Natalie had so many questions, and one way to get answers. Hurrying after Francisco, she followed him inside.

If Francisco was up to something, she still saw no sign of it. He stood in the middle of a dusty marble hallway, looking up and around at the grand room. The ceiling was made of glass, and old leaves had caught here and there and blotted out some of the sunlight. A large staircase swept up and around, going up several floors.

It was impressive, but the whole house smelled musty and Natalie wrinkled her nose as her friends joined them.

"I believe that what we seek will be upstairs, but, please, let me go first in case any of the steps have rotted or grown weak." Francisco didn't wait for anyone to object, but stepped onto the green carpeted staircase and ascended, one careful step at a time.

Lucas beat Natalie to follow the werewolf up the stairs, but she followed as soon as she dared, stepping almost exactly where he did and wincing every time the stairs creaked.

Alia came next and seemed to make no noise, her elven footsteps light and even. That was one stereotype that appeared to hold. Francisco stopped on the next floor and went through a large archway. It led to a carpeted hallway with large windows down one side and doors off the other.

A courtyard lay to the side of the house, as unkempt as the rest of the grounds had become, but Francisco wasn't paying it any attention. His eyes were fixed on the doorways as he counted. The second doorway had large claw marks in the wood, as if an animal had been pulled through and grabbed on to hold themselves firm but not succeeded.

Natalie's eyes went wide when she spotted it, but Francisco merely ran one hand over the door frame and carried on to the next. This door stood closed, but again the werewolf pulled out the key and unlocked it.

He pushed inside to reveal a large library or study with a desk at the far end as well as several tables. All the walls were lined with books, and several were out on the tables, open as if they had been flipped through recently.

Alia moved over to the nearest stack. All the books were in a language that Natalie had never seen before.

"Elvish?" she asked.

Alia shook her head but didn't explain. Whatever language it was, no one was going to tell Natalie. She watched the young elf read though, her mouth moving as her eyes scanned the page. Alia soon frowned, and a moment later she picked up the book and took it to a nearby seat to sit down and continue.

Not wanting to disturb the elf when she was clearly reading something important, Natalie moved closer to

Francisco instead. Lucas jumped up onto the chair in front of the main desk and sat, making it look as if this were his study.

Francisco was already also absorbed in a book and reading with a frown on his face.

"Please don't tell me that it's not here," Lucas begged.

"It would appear that this is not the great library that the werewolf put together on these particular artifacts. So the artifacts themselves will be with the great library hopefully, or we will be able to find the whereabouts there." The frustration and sadness in Francisco's voice were unmistakable. This wasn't what he'd wanted either.

"So where is the great library?" Natalie asked.

"That is what I hope to find from these books, *ma chère*. But there is a lot to look through, and unfortunately, your help can only get me this far. I must do this part myself."

She nodded and backed up, going to look at other books anyway and see if she stumbled upon something in English, or at least a language that wasn't tied to a magical language and she might have a chance of translating. There were so many books with titles she couldn't read, but the room was wonderful anyway.

She inhaled, taking in the old leather and pages smell. It was one of the best scents in the world, and it reminded her of one of the few good things about growing up. Her mother had been well connected, and one of their family friends had taken pride in their library. Natalie had loved it when they visited. She'd spent many rainy afternoons there reading while her parents talked in the background.

It was one of the few times when no one would encourage her to do anything else or be anywhere else. Her mother had wanted to talk, and Natalie had stayed quiet and out of the way and let it happen. She never nagged her mother about leaving or getting bored. Everyone had been happy.

Sitting to one side, Alia continued to read, flipping through a book almost aggressively, as if she couldn't absorb the information fast enough, but her frown had grown deeper. Whatever she was reading, it was bothering her. Natalie considered going to her and asking what it was about, but she feared the intrusion wouldn't be welcome.

Instead, she made the mental note to ask the elf about it later if a good moment came up, when Alia might be more likely to feel as if she could talk about it.

Rich and Lucas stayed up at the far end of the study. Rich stared out at the view and the town in front of them. The house was partway up the hill, and Natalie knew it would be worth seeing from further up.

Deciding that there weren't any books in a language she could read, Natalie moved to the door to continue exploring the rest of the house.

"I wouldn't go wandering around if I were you, *ma chère*," Francisco called from over by the desk. "Some of these ancient houses have magic protecting certain areas. As a human, you could get yourself into…trouble."

Natalie froze. They already had one cursed member and didn't need another. So she moved back toward the window, intending to join Rich at the good view. If she could do nothing to find it from higher up, she could at least enjoy it from here.

With a sigh, Francisco put down a book and looked for

another one. It didn't look like this was going to be swift, and it made Natalie wish they'd thought of bringing lunch with them.

After a few minutes, she spotted movement down in the grounds of the house.

"Enforcers," Rich stated a fraction before Natalie was about to state the same thing. There were four of them coming up to the house. One of them was carrying something and looked wary.

Francisco froze as Alia got up. This was a huge problem.

CHAPTER TWENTY-FIVE

As one, all of them moved away. Alia frowned. She snapped what she had been reading shut with a bang but noticed Francisco bringing the book he had been looking through with him. He tucked it into the back of his pants and covered it with his jacket as he did. She guessed that some magic artifact activated a moment later, because the outline of it under his clothes vanished. Some small Unplace holder or something?

She didn't waste time checking as they all hurried toward the steps to find a back route out of the house. They were about to go through the archway when Lucas paused and turned back.

The clatter of boots on the marble floor let them know that they were too late. They turned and hurried back the other way.

"There should be some servants' stairs at this far end," Francisco whispered.

It was all they could hope for, but Alia continued to feel distracted. It was as if it didn't matter that the enforcers had found them. Her mind was still on what she'd read. She'd been taught so many things about the werewolves, and if the book she'd been reading was correct, a lot of it was wrong. It even talked about how the elves and the rest of the magical races that served them had covered up the truth.

Had her own race lied to her about the evilness of werewolves and how greedy they had become?

The account she had heard must have been wrong. Too much made sense now, and too much matched with the memories she had as a child. Sadly, what she knew of wealthier elves fit with what the book said.

If she'd had anywhere to put it, she would have taken it too, but she'd have to hope she could come back or find another way to get the truth. Now, she had to focus on getting them all out of there and away from the enforcers.

The other end of the wing revealed a smaller set of stairs. They were a few steps down when the door at the bottom opened and more enforcers appeared.

Hoping they hadn't been seen, they turned to go up instead of down as quietly as they could. It wasn't going well so far, and Alia feared they would trigger some magic at any moment.

To her surprise, Francisco insisted on going first. He scooped up Lucas and handed him to Natalie. Alia brought up the rear, reaching for the stone tool that she'd found in the catacombs under the cathedral. It might work on the walls of the house, or at least buy them some time or perhaps help them get around a cursed door.

She turned it on but didn't use it, slipping it onto one hand as the footfalls from the enforcers below stopped after the first flight. It gave her and her friends a window to get free and find another way down and out.

It bothered her that they were going in the wrong direction as they reached yet another floor. The doorway to the main wing stood open, and they rushed through. All the doors to their left were shut and locked. Francisco and Alia only needed to move toward the first one to feel the magic humming off it in waves.

Alia stopped Natalie before she could try the handle.

"Trust me, you don't want to do that."

The human backed up, gulping as if she'd brushed with death. Alia didn't know if she had or hadn't, but didn't want to find out.

They rushed along, feeling the magic over all the doors. Another archway ahead showed them the main stairwell, but they heard people talking that way too. Rich looked out the windows to the courtyard long enough to see that there were more enforcers out there as well. They had come in force.

Alia moved to the wall of one of the bedrooms and lifted her device. It didn't take her long to make an opening that let her through. Natalie pulled out the other and hesitated for a second. When she was unable to turn it on, she handed it back to the werewolf.

Half an hour earlier, Alia would have stopped her, but not now. Now she knew Francisco could be trusted. He *did* want to restore his race, and he had every right to.

Between the two of them, they managed to make a hole big enough so they could all get through and into the bedroom beyond. It was huge and had once been the master suite for a werewolf with expensive taste in décor.

A fireplace stood against the left wall, and a large four-post bed stood against the opposite wall.

The curtains were still closed across the far window, but time and neglect had allowed moths to eat little holes, and a strange dappled light filtered through. They were stuck. There was nowhere for them to go after that, and barely time for Alia to close the wall before they were discovered.

"They will work out that we're in here eventually," Francisco pointed out. "There is no other way. You must save yourselves by turning me in."

"We can't do that," Natalie protested instantly, looking as if she might burst into tears at any moment.

Normally, Alia wouldn't have cared about what was necessary, but she agreed with Natalie this time. She didn't voice it aloud, though.

"I'm with Natalie on this one, Francisco," Rich added. "We can't turn you in. Even if we didn't like you, we need you. Lucas is still a cat."

"I know that the three of you can keep going. This house and the study are open to you. You can find what you need to help your friend from here. Thank you for all you have done to aid me."

Alia didn't open the hole in the wall back up. This felt wrong, and she understood everyone's hesitation.

"Come, Alia. It would be fitting for you to be the one to arrest me." Francisco pulled out some handcuffs, offering them to her so she could use them on him. "I know you have been eager to do this since the beginning, *ma chère.*"

Although it wasn't what she wanted to do anymore, she didn't want him to know quite how much he had charmed her as well. Deliberately and with as much precision as she could muster, she put the handcuffs on him, grateful that this set was real, non-magical, and didn't have any easy way out of them that she could detect.

When the cuffs were on the werewolf, she moved back to the wall and reopened the hole. She pretended not to notice that Francisco hadn't given Natalie back the stone manipulating device that he had fought them with in the cemetery. If he found a way to smuggle that into wherever they were taking him and got out, she wasn't sure she minded anymore.

Once they were on the other side of the wall again, they moved as a group, all of them around Francisco as if they were an escort squad. Alia led the way, but she didn't have to take him far before the enforcers spotted him.

"Got him for you," she reported as soon as she saw them, wanting to make sure they understood he was being handed over.

Although it was probably an act, Francisco no longer wore the charming smile or held his head high. He appeared slumped, his face downcast and his movements more sluggish.

"This is the werewolf?" The enforcer's English came out a little stilted and his accent was heavy.

"Yes, this is the criminal they want in Paris."

"Good. We will take him from here. You can return to the department who hired you," another enforcer instructed. He appeared to be more in charge as he came hurrying up the stairs.

Alia didn't fight it, although this didn't feel right

anymore. She kept to one side and let Rich step forward to interact with the enforcers as if he were in charge.

They exchanged a few words as Alia watched Francisco. He acted resigned to everything and willing to let the enforcers take him away, harmless and tired of it all. When he thought no one was looking, however, he flicked Natalie a wink.

It gave Alia some hope that he would be okay and that if nothing else, he didn't blame them for how this had ended. It was over now. Now they had to go back to looking for a cure for Lucas on their own. Francisco had helped them get closer, and that was something to be very grateful for.

The enforcers didn't insist they leave. They just took Francisco and packed up, letting Alia and the others make their way back to the floor below where the study was. Although Alia was tempted to keep reading the book she'd found, she put it in her bag instead, emboldened by seeing Francisco take one of the books. If it was as true an account of old events as she thought it was, she wanted to make copies of it. She wanted to make sure more of the magical community knew.

Now wasn't the time for personal reflection, however. They needed to figure out their next step.

CHAPTER TWENTY-SIX

Rich sank into the chair by the window, feeling deflated. This wasn't how he had imagined the day would go. He'd been on the lookout for Francisco to double cross them. Hoped Lucas might return to being human. Or even that they would have to continue down a rabbit hole. Losing Francisco to the enforcers hadn't been something he'd expected.

They hadn't been on the radar. They should have been free of the magic police.

Instead, they were sitting in a study with a whole pile of books in languages that most of them didn't read, and trying to find a way to get to a library. It was almost ironic, given the number of books around them. There were more in here than the library he'd gone to in the small town where he'd grown up.

The difference was that most of these appeared to be handwritten, old, and not fiction.

Lucas sat on the edge of the desk in one of the bars of sunlight that streamed across it and started licking a paw.

He wasn't talking to them anywhere near as much as he used to and it was a worrying sign.

Alia was browsing one section of books with Natalie, the latter having asked if there were any she might be able to read. So far, they weren't having any luck pinpointing anything.

There were a few books in European languages, but they were the few fiction stories and weren't going to have any information about the artifact that might save Lucas. Everything else was in one of the three main languages of the magical races: Elven, Were, and Dwarven. Alia could read the first two well enough and the third a little.

It was going to be slow going unless they could find a way to understand the pages. Maybe they could scan them in somehow. Rich considered pulling his phone out to look something up that might be a quick document scanner. If Alia could show them how to link to some dictionary for the magical languages, it might work.

Of course, they would be slower than Alia, but it would also serve to preserve some of these books. He sighed as he thought about how it wouldn't be easy to get what he needed in the town below them. This wasn't a big place. He doubted they had a tech store of any kind. And by the time they had something delivered and had everything set up, Alia was likely to have read all the relevant books already.

"Are you going to help at all?" Natalie asked with a slight bite to her words.

Rich raised his eyebrows. She was probably annoyed because they were all stuck and there wasn't a lot that any of them could do, but he explained his line of thinking anyway.

"It's an idea I think would work if we had more time," Alia agreed. "And there are a lot of books here that I've never seen before. Once we have the reward money for Francisco, I think we should consider coming back here to scan them all in anyway."

"Really?" Rich liked the appreciation Alia had for his suggestion. He'd felt as if she'd been disappointed in all of them lately, especially him, for being charmed by the werewolf.

"Yes. If nothing else, the information in them could be reprinted and sold." Her grin grew wider as she spoke, and Natalie chuckled softly.

Even Rich couldn't help but smile as he also shook his head. It was always funny to think of Alia as being the kind of person to do similar things as Francisco, like liberate things from one person to give or sell to another because, in her opinion, the world was a better place in some way or another for her having done so.

It was a shady thing to do in some ways. There was no final authority to make sure the morality behind the decisions was sound. He could understand why it might be necessary in some circumstances, though. If those in power were as corrupt as some of the stories Alia and Francisco had shared, then Rich agreed with the pair of them about what they were doing.

"What about the glasses?" Natalie mused as she took them off and held them out. "If it's going to take too long to get what we need to scan all the books, but there are databases we can hook into to help translate the books, then what if we connect these to the glasses and modify the code to show a direct translation overlay or something?"

Rich tilted his head to the side as he thought about it, but ultimately shook his head. He could do that, but they still hadn't had the time to figure out why the glasses could do the things they were doing in the first place. And the last time he'd had to modify them, it had been…an experience.

The truth was that the best person to get the glasses to help them was currently washing his face with paws and then licking the dirt off those very paws. It didn't bode well for the situation.

Natalie sat in another chair and Alia followed. The pair of them looked utterly defeated.

"There's no point in us sitting here and being miserable," Rich proposed. "There was a pub down the road. Why don't we go get food and a drink or two and figure out what we're going to do next?"

The three of them looked at each other for a bit and, as one, stood. It wasn't a hard decision. They couldn't do much here and it made no sense to stay in a house so full of magic that it liked to attack intruders. If there were any books that would help here, they were going to need to find them another day and in another way.

The group kept close to each other, with Natalie carrying Lucas again, and left the house. At the front door, Alia hesitated, frowning at the lock. She knelt in front of it to inspect it more closely.

"Okay, I could pick this if we wanted to come back. And there doesn't seem to be any magic on it anymore." Alia closed the door and they walked down the driveway and away from the house.

It was a very different atmosphere than it had been

when they'd arrived, and the member they were missing was very noticeable. They needed the pick-me-up of some good pub food and drinks.

Rich led them back down to where he'd noticed the pub and they trooped inside. Natalie did her best to not make Lucas obvious. She and Alia found a table while Rich went to the bar to attempt an order. The guy behind the bar seemed happy to practice his English, and made the task of ordering food and a round of drinks easier than Rich had feared.

Before long, they were sitting at a round table in the corner of the quiet pub. They had three empty plates in front of them and they were deep into their second beers each.

Having some food in their stomachs and with the alcohol to take the edge off, the three of them were relaxed for the first time in what felt like weeks. Despite the feeling of calm that came with sitting down to a good meal, though, they were still clearly sad, and no one had much to say. Lucas was sitting on Natalie's lap. The pub owner didn't care that he was there and had even given them a saucer so they could share a drink with him. It amused everyone to see him lapping up some of Rich's beer, but they'd already had to cut him off.

"We need Francisco," Alia pointed out a few minutes into a silence that appeared to stretch across the room and added to the air of despair. "He had some idea of what he was looking for, and this is his native language."

"But he's answering for his crimes." Natalie sighed and sat back, and for the first time Rich wondered if Alia's offhand comment was her way of saying she didn't mind what he'd done anymore.

"But we need him, and he kept his word to us. Even gave himself up to keep it a secret that he had been working with us. That means something to me." Rich leaned forward and stroked Lucas, hoping to encourage him to join in this conversation.

"I'm tired of being a cat, either way." It was all Lucas said and it was clearly all he was going to offer as he curled up against a stack of books and put his head down on his paws. Rich continued to give him gentle head scritches, not sure how else to reassure his friend that they were aware of his plight and trying their hardest to do something about it.

Natalie sighed and shook her head, but then a grin stole across her face. "We do have that stone-bending thingy still. Could we break him out of some kind of prison?"

It wasn't long before Alia was returning the expression and lifting the device Natalie was referring to.

They looked at Rich as if this was his decision. He thought about it. If they were caught doing it, they could get into a lot of trouble. Then he looked at Lucas, and he knew the answer. They had to try. Because they weren't getting Lucas back any other way.

"Okay," he agreed. "Let's figure out how we're going to get Francisco back before he's taken too far away from us. And let's try and be cool about it."

"Cool about it?"

"Yeah, do it with style, like in one of those heist movies." Rich grinned as Alia shook her head and Natalie chuckled. Heist movie it was.

CHAPTER TWENTY-SEVEN

Alia stared at Rich and Natalie as it dawned on her that they were serious. She looked at the empty beer glasses on the table, checking how much they had both had and wondered if that might have something to do with it, but although the three of them had drunk plenty between them, it wasn't a large amount per person yet.

They were sober enough.

"Okay, let me get this straight. Because Francisco is the only person who can help us save Lucas and because we suspect that he might be innocent you want to break him out of jail and you want my help with magic to do it?"

"Yes," Natalie confirmed. "And we know that you're fine with that because you've been sitting there thinking about it as well for the past few minutes rather than telling us we're idiots and you never want to talk to us again."

Although Alia would hate to admit it, Natalie had a point. It was something she was fine with. She had been thinking of it, and she knew she'd put the idea in their heads. They needed the werewolf, and she'd mentioned it first.

Actually breaking him out was going to be another matter.

"They'll hold him for a while somewhere nearby, until they know where he's going to be charged and for what crimes. And then he'll be extradited." Alia wasn't sure how she knew all this, but she was grateful she'd spent enough time with other criminals to have the knowledge she needed now.

"We need to get him out before then." Rich sat forward and took another swig of beer.

"Agreed. We should move sooner rather than later. They'd expect any escape plans to happen when he's being moved, not before. The enforcers here will be less skilled. They won't have as many checks and systems in place here."

"So a rushed movie heist. We're smart enough for that, right?"

"Probably. Enforcers… If they're anything like the ones in the US, it's one of the jobs magic users do if they're not much good at doing other jobs with magic. The weaker ones who are bitter about not being as good."

"So we've got some jaded and not particularly sharp enforcers and no way of knowing which kind we're going to get."

"Pretty much." Alia reached for her phone to research the enforcer prison in the town. It wouldn't be very big, but if they had an old derelict werewolf mansion in town, they would have some sort of holding area too.

As she expected, it was tiny, only a few cells by the

looks of the outside the building. There wasn't any more easily accessible information, however.

Although Alia didn't expect to get a result, she reached out to a few of her old contacts and asked if they could get her more information on the prison. It was a long shot when they weren't in the same country, but sometimes someone knew somebody who knew another person and then they could get what you needed.

It was worth a try.

"Natalie is right, with the device we've got, I might be able to help create an escape route, but I'm going to need a distraction and we need to make sure that we're not seen. While so far we haven't appeared to break any laws, if they know that we're involved in breaking him out of prison, we all go from skirting the edges of the law to actually breaking it."

"I can help then, 'cause if this works I won't be a cat much longer afterward and they'll never recognize me." Lucas' words were slurred before he stretched and settled down on Natalie's lap.

"Can you do some fancy stuff with the tech again?" Alia asked Rich. "Scramble cameras, that kind of thing?"

Rich looked thoughtful. "I might be able to jam them or something, but then they'll know Francisco had help."

"Unless we send Lucas in," Natalie suggested. "If he goes in, then Francisco will know we're coming and we can make it look like it originates with him."

This made Rich think, and he reached for his rucksack to pull out his laptop.

They had to ask the pub owner if they could use the

Wi-Fi, then bought another round of drinks to repay his kindness when he let them use the private one.

Rich got to work, and Alia continued to search for the information she needed to work out where Francisco was likely to be held. Lucas repeated his offer to be a little scout, slurring his words and stumbling over his ideas and making Natalie giggle.

"We've got the glasses too," she pointed out when Alia worried about not knowing if any of the enforcers were competent mages or if they could pick up on anything from far away.

"And we still need a distraction," Rich added, still tapping away on his keyboard. Now and then he reached into his bag and pulled out a bit of hardware or something he plugged into the laptop.

He was right, but that left Natalie, and Alia could only think of one way the woman might be able to get them the information they needed.

"We need you to go into the enforcer building and flirt," Alia told Natalie a few seconds later.

Natalie gulped and her eyes widened.

"Nope. Have you seen me flirt?"

"Yes, you're bad at it, but you need to do it anyway. Everyone else is going to be busy with another part of the plan and those enforcers were pretty much all male."

Natalie rolled her eyes. "You know that doesn't mean they all swing my way, right?"

"Good point, but you're still our best bet. And you'll be a distraction either way."

"Touché. Okay, if I must, but I am making it very clear

that I do this under protest. I don't want to be flirting with anyone and I definitely don't want to succeed."

Rich chuckled and Alia let herself grin slightly. They sort of had a plan, and that meant they were going to do this. Bust someone out of magic prison. Once again, Alia marveled at the group she was with. In the past, if anyone she'd worked with had gotten themselves caught for anything, they'd been cut loose.

It was one of those unspoken rules. No one was going to risk their neck any more than they had to. If you got caught you were on your own. That meant there were no elaborate breakouts or even hastily planned ones over beers at the pub. Just the ever-nagging doubt in the back of your head that you were screwed if you got caught and couldn't get yourself out of it.

Someone had told Alia once that the real skill was knowing when to stop. Knowing when you'd run your luck out and your ability to talk your way out of a problem. Alia had begun to get to that point in the US, but it hadn't occurred to her that she could create a second chance in another country.

Everyone in France had assumed she was honorable and that she had been put on the case because she had the right skills. They hadn't liked having humans around or that she was an elf, but that was nothing new. Her possible crimes hadn't followed her, though, and it made it more understandable why Francisco had moved around.

"Okay," Rich began but then paused for a moment, staring at his computer screen. Alia raised her eyebrows. Finally he went on, "I think it's done and ready to go."

"You *think*?" she asked. "I think being sure would be helpful."

"There's a couple of ways we can test it," he explained. "Then I'll be sure."

Rich held out the small device he'd made and scrutinized Lucas for where they might be able to hide it on him.

"We could tie it around his neck on a sort of collar, try and make it look like one of those things that open cat flaps," Natalie suggested as she helped turn Lucas around.

"You're not putting that thing on me," Lucas protested, but Natalie already had a good grip on him and wouldn't let go.

Alia handed Rich some ribbon to tie it with, and before Lucas could do anything but grumble and wriggle uselessly against Natalie, Rich had it tied around his neck, hanging like a collar underneath.

"There." He sat back and picked his laptop back up again. "Now we can test it."

Natalie let go of the cat and Lucas jumped down to the floor. He didn't look steady on his feet when he looked up at Rich, resigned.

"Point me in the right direction and let's see if we can cause some chaos."

Rich grinned and gave him some instructions. He sent him over to the TV in one corner of the pub and around the bar and back. Any electronics Lucas and the device got close to stopped working properly. Alia grinned. This was perfect.

She got up as soon as Lucas was back with Natalie. "Right. We're ready and we've taken so long coming up with this plan that we need to get on with it sooner rather than later. We're not risking them moving him later tonight."

There wasn't an argument from the others as Rich packed up everything. The three of them looked at each other, downed the last of their pints and made their way out into the town again.

It still wasn't quite dark, but things were beginning to wind down for the day. Everywhere was getting more quiet and the light would continue to fade. Perfect for a prison break.

CHAPTER TWENTY-EIGHT

With a stomach trying to tie itself in one very large knot and palms that were sweaty even after wiping them on her jeans for the third time, Natalie approached the enforcers' office. She was the one who had to start this whole plan and it was the worst part of the whole idea.

Flirt? They wanted her to flirt. It wasn't her strong suit. In high school, she hadn't been one of the girls all the guys were interested in. A little too geeky to be cool and not geeky enough for them to come to her for homework help. It was the worst position to be in.

It helped to remind herself that she didn't have to do this well, just for long enough. Unless, of course, she did this so badly that they had her removed from the premises for disturbing the peace.

She had the glasses on, which gave her a certain level of confidence. If nothing else, she could feed information to Alia, who was listening to everything on the phone that was in Natalie's pocket and connected to a Bluetooth earpiece.

Natalie pushed open the door and strode inside. She stopped and looked around the room, making her eyes go wider as if she were a little scared and not sure what to do. There were three people inside: two men sitting off to one side at desks and another at what looked like a guard post.

"Ummm… Do any of you three speak English?" she asked, letting some of her nerves and fear out. She gulped as they all looked at her.

None of them spoke, so she took a step forward, having held the door open the entire time, hoping to give Lucas a moment to sneak in now that they were all looking at her.

"Oh, my, do you work out?" she asked. She was pointing to the most muscular of the three, the guard by the back of the room and near what must have been the prison cells.

Everyone looked in his direction, and even he looked at himself, surprised and unsure what she was saying. Behind her, Natalie hoped Lucas was taking the opportunity to rush in unnoticed.

As she let go of the door and glanced back to let it swing shut, she caught the end of his tail as he darted through and then behind a desk. Now that part of her job was done, she relaxed a little and strode forward.

"Are you the enforcers that have Francisco the were-wolf?" she asked.

This time the guard nodded and glanced at the cells. The information in her goggles told her that this was a half-elf and half-human and also a warlock, but not a very powerful one

"Oh, he's down there?" She pointed again, but the warlock frowned and glanced at his companions, clearly not enjoying her attention right now.

She bit her lip and tried to think of how she could distract him so Lucas could run down toward Francisco.

"Do you speak English, sir? I need help and you look as if you're the sort of hero I need." She batted her eyelashes a couple of times, hoping she was coming off more subtle than she felt. "Did the werewolf come in with any magic items? I've had one stolen off me and I haven't seen it since we helped you catch him."

Her words appeared to have some impact on the man. He stood straighter.

"We didn't find anything particularly on him," the guard reported in a thick accent. "Not magic anyway."

Natalie sighed and shook her head but continued to walk closer. She angled toward the back of the room and away from the cells. She wanted all eyes on her now.

"Oh... I don't know what I'm going to do. It wasn't really mine and you seem like such a...such a...strong and...well-built man. I mean, I'm sure that you know how to solve all sorts of problems." As Natalie waffled and tried to think of some smooth line about his mental skill, she saw Lucas finally run for it and head for Francisco's cell.

At this angle, she could see through an open doorway to the cells and saw Francisco's arms reach through the bars to pick Lucas up. That was one part of the equation solved.

"I'm sorry, miss, we didn't find anything."

Natalie sighed and looked like she might cry.

"But you're clearly so clever and wonderful. If this werewolf doesn't have it then I don't know where it is. Can I report it missing?"

She tried to flutter her eyelashes again while also

looking sad, but she guessed she just came across as weird. The guy opposite her cocked an appraising eyebrow.

In her earpiece, she thought she heard Rich laughing.

"She really is bad at flirting, isn't she," Alia muttered. Natalie wanted to respond and tell the elf to get in here and try it herself.

"Okay, miss. Why don't you come and sit down, and we will try to help you. Is this artifact dangerous?" The guard got her attention again and reminded her that she needed to keep him distracted, not be distracted herself.

"I didn't think it was, but I suppose it might be. Am I in trouble? I really didn't mean for something to happen. I just thought that you might be able to help. You really do look so strong and confident sitting here and it's been a nightmare of a few days trying to—"

Natalie was interrupted by the loud sound of a clanging alarm from down the corridor and in the cell area.

She screamed, and didn't have to entirely fake her emotional state to make it sound realistic. All three men jumped up and checked on her rather than going to the cells.

"Please stay here, miss, or return to your accommodation and come back later." The guard turned and headed toward the danger.

More laughter rang in her ear despite the pursuit now heading Francisco's way. "What's going on?" she asked, hoping that Alia would realize that the question was meant for her and respond.

"Francisco is out of his cell, but the enforcers had an alarm on him, and it triggered the moment he stepped out.

He's running. We need you and the glasses out here," Alia explained, also sounding out of breath.

A moment later, Lucas ran toward her, darting between the legs of the enforcers as they ran after the werewolf and tried to stop him from escaping. She resisted the urge to pick him up again and instead hurried away to open the front door and run for it. It was time to get a werewolf out of the prison and back on the hunt for this great library.

CHAPTER TWENTY-NINE

A grin spread across Rich's face as the werewolf appeared at the edge of the building, coming out of the hole Alia had made earlier. She was still using her magic to make pathways through the town for him.

They needed to get out of the town before the enforcers could catch up to them again, and that wasn't going to be easy now they'd triggered the alarm.

Francisco went running as he put the earpiece in his ear that Alia had tied onto Lucas' collar.

He joined in the phone call. "My friends, your help is most useful in this matter. I confess I had expected you all to head on your merry way."

"We figured you could do with a hand, and we make a good team," Rich replied, not mentioning that he had been the most reluctant of all of them when it came to the plan and getting him out.

"They should not see you all helping me," he cautioned as he ran off into the trees away from them and the city.

A few seconds later, Lucas ran around the corner with Natalie a few yards behind him. They came straight to Alia and Rich where they were hiding in the shadows behind the building. They watched the enforcers come out of the hole, spot the fleeing werewolf ahead, and give chase.

The two enforcers called things to each other, but they weren't in English. The guard came next, carrying something that looked like a scanner of sorts.

"Looks like they still have a tracker on you," Natalie warned Francisco. Her glasses must have told her what the item was. "Something magical, 'cause the glasses are picking up on it. I have a sort of arrow in my vision pointing you out with coordinates attached to it."

"Thank you, *ma chère*. Most kind of you. I will destroy it momentarily, although I am not entirely sure of the merit while they can still see me to chase anyway."

"We'll see what we can do," Alia put in. She looked at Natalie and instructed, "Go to the train station and buy tickets for whatever train is leaving in half an hour. Then buy tickets for whatever train is leaving five minutes after that, and use cash."

Natalie grinned as she took off the glasses and handed them to Rich. It was time to get everyone out of there.

"Half an hour. I will be there, my friends." Francisco continued running, and the mic picked up his breathing as Rich put on the glasses and Lucas ran after everyone.

Rich saw the arrow that Natalie had mentioned, a moving target on the werewolf's back. No doubt this was the system tapping into the information that the guard had. Somehow, they had to block it, get Francisco out of sight, and get everyone to the train station in half an hour. He hoped Alia had a plan, because he didn't.

It seemed Lucas was going to help, however. He ran at the guard, and when he was close to him, Rich's device took effect. The man slowed and shook his device.

"How are we going to help?" Rich asked Alia as she strapped on the stone device again and ran to the left of the guard and up an incline toward the back of town.

"Guide Francisco through the woods and up to the mansion again. Head there and get the tracker off him. Lucas can keep jamming their signal, and I'm going to slow the enforcers down." Alia ran off, manipulating the ground from behind the guard.

The enforcer tripped as the rock shifted and sent him tumbling forward. It gave Alia a window to run ahead, staying out of sight as the guard focused on his device now, unable to see his colleagues or the werewolf.

Rich ran up another street, accepting that they were going to have to split up. He encouraged Francisco to turn a little more to the left as well. He pulled out his phone and used the map on that to help the werewolf find a path to the mansion, while he went via a back way.

Alia swore. "These enforcers really don't want to give up and this device isn't working from so far away. We need to buy him some time another way."

"Get to the house as well," Natalie suggested. "If there's only three of them and you can open walls, you can play cat-and-mouse and get them to trigger some of the magic." A train horn blew in the background and they had to listen as she ordered the tickets they needed.

"Once again, the young woman shows she has the brains," Francisco replied. "All of us to the house and Lucas to stop them tracking properly." It was a gleeful statement, and the werewolf was in high spirits, if out of breath

Alia was the first to reach the house. She could start working on opening walls and shutting doors, making it difficult to get in any way they didn't want. Rich was next, and he dove inside after her, going through the back and the kitchen.

It was a room they hadn't seen the first time, but he noticed a fridge in one corner, and some food on a sideboard. It was rotted and had been eaten by flies until there was almost nothing left. Although he'd have expected it to smell, it didn't anymore.

Alia left the opening for Francisco for now. She ran to the front door and sealed it, then brought some brick out behind the door and made the house shift and move. She did the same with other doors and opened a few other holes until Rich lost track of everything she was doing.

All the while, Rich directed the werewolf closer.

"I must say, these two enforcers have got legs on them. It's not every day that such fellows can keep up."

"They're probably using magic," Alia guessed.

"At this rate, you're going to all need to use magic," Natalie's voice was a little more shrill than usual. "You've got fifteen minutes until the first train."

"We'll be there, *ma chère*. Have some faith in the skill of so many masterminds. It is the five of us versus these three, and they do not possess our wits."

Rich was glad that someone still felt upbeat about this. He followed Alia into yet another room.

"That one is booby-trapped," Rich murmured when the glasses fed him information on the door Alia was about to open.

She grinned.

"Perfect. Let's hope it's something nasty."

"Oh, given the house owner, it's likely to be quite delightful." Francisco sounded excited, and Rich looked at Alia, feeling almost scared of him for the first time ever.

"I don't think delightful means what you think it does," Rich replied.

There were chuckles all around, and Rich felt like, if nothing else, he had helped to lighten the mood. He had, but they still had to get Francisco away from the enforcers.

"Almost there," Francisco called a moment later. Rich pulled out his phone again to get a handle on where the others were. Once Lucas joined them with the new device, it wouldn't work and he wouldn't even necessarily be able to get the glasses to function until it was disabled.

Before long, Francisco came through the gap in the kitchen wall, and Alia rushed over to help get the gap closed behind him. Between the two of them, the hole was closed fast.

"This way." Alia led them all deeper into the house.

Rich felt a bit like a spare wheel with the large werewolf smiling and helping. The two of them made the walls move and open and close for them, and they hurried through the house, making it look like they were going in a direction they weren't and leading the two enforcers deeper and deeper.

Right at the last minute, the three of them took a different route, creating the illusion that they were going into one of the rooms that had a cursed door then sneaking back the way they'd come. They went through premade holes and closed them behind them.

A few seconds later, someone yelped, followed by a loud clatter. They all paused for a moment, looking back to where the enforcers must have set off some cursed trap.

"We've really got to hurry," Rich called as he looked at the time. They didn't have long to get on the right train. He still hadn't seen Lucas anywhere, and the third enforcer was nowhere to be seen.

They were coming back around to the rear door when the cat ran in through a small hole in a door panel that one of the enforcers must have made.

"You don't want to go that way," Lucas reported as soon as he saw them. "Out the front and we should be good to go."

"Do you want to explain?" Rich asked as he scooped the cat up and into his arms.

"It turns out that there's some cursed stuff out the back too." Lucas panted, clearly exhausted from whatever he had been doing.

Francisco clapped his hands together in delight and rushed toward the front door as if this was the beginning of an exciting party.

This time, the werewolf simply opened the door. Nothing bad happened, and they hurried out into the front yard.

They ran toward the train station. Some streetlamps had come on, and Rich thought they shouldn't be seen together if they could help it. They had no way to know if more enforcers had been called as backup, or if the first three would be able to get out of the house and after them.

Rich told Francisco to run one way as he, Alia, and Lucas took a parallel route.

Natalie's urgent voice came over the call they still had open with her. "You guys need to really hurry. The train is now pulling into the station. It's going to pause for a few minutes, but you've got to really hustle."

"We will be there, *ma chère*. Do not fret for us." Francisco hurried ahead of them. The tracker in him would still be making it clear to anyone with the right technology where he was. Rich hoped he had a plan for what to do with that, but he himself had to focus on giving directions and getting everyone to the train station.

The building came up in front of them. Their paths had to come back together again, but Francisco was running faster than the other three of them, helped by not having to hold an exhausted cat and follow a map at the same time.

He ran in over a hundred yards ahead of them, and Natalie took over the directions, guiding him to the platform of the train she was on. Alia found some extra oomph from somewhere and powered ahead of Rich as well. It was all he could do at that point to hold onto the cat and his phone and keep going.

As the ache in Rich's legs grew and he couldn't help but slow, Francisco made it to the train. Rich heard Natalie greeting him in person and their voices coming across the call.

Alia came close, but the train pulled off before she could get on. Rich never had a chance.

"Okay guys, we have a problem."

"Get the second train," Francisco suggested. "We'll be with you shortly. I'm sure Natalie can assist me in getting rid of this tracker."

Rich wanted to object, but it was the only plan open to them.

CHAPTER THIRTY

No matter what Natalie did, she couldn't shake her stomach full of nerves. It twisted and turned in her gut like a knife and she didn't know what to do to make herself feel better. She was stuck on a train with Francisco, watching her friends disappear into the distance.

The werewolf had told them to get the second train and said something about a tracker, but she felt helpless.

"Come, Natalie, let us get somewhere out of the prying eyes of others." Francisco grabbed her hand and pulled her toward the small restroom on the train.

This didn't make her feel any better. As soon as they were inside and the door was shut, Natalie tried to back up against the far wall, wondering what on earth the werewolf could be thinking and hoping that she hadn't just gotten herself killed.

"I need your help, *ma chère*." He pulled something seemingly out of the thin air from behind his back. The strange triangle made of some ornate carved metal seemed to come to life in his hand, glowing with a pulsing light.

"What do you want me to do with that?" she asked when he held it out to her.

"Help me locate and remove this tracker. I have tried to find it myself and I cannot."

Natalie frowned but she took the small thing and held two of the points between her thumb and forefinger like he showed her. Instantly, it seemed to connect with her.

"Don't worry, it is just picking up on the magic ability in you. You must have a little fae ancestry to be able to do that, even if it is not something you've taken to naturally."

"I'm just hoping I don't hurt you," she fretted as he turned his back on her.

"It cannot be as painful as your flirting earlier, *ma chère*. But do not fret. You cannot harm me, but we need to be fast. We need to get off at the next stop and make our way back to your friends."

Natalie didn't need the pressure, but she focused on the device and his instructions to move it over all the skin where he couldn't see to move it over himself. She didn't need to get too close, but it was close enough and personal enough that as she moved lower, she felt her cheeks flushing.

When she was near his lower back, she was saved from further embarrassment by the device starting to flash.

"Ah, you have discovered it. Move it around until the flashing grows closer together and becomes a constant light, then you are right above it."

Natalie didn't find this part of the instruction quite as easy. The device was sensitive enough that getting it in exactly the right place was hard, especially on a moving train that was jolting them around. Finally, she got it there.

"Now activate the triangle by pushing the button and letting the magic flow. As you did when you hurled rocks at me."

Grinning at the memory of trying to hit the werewolf with rocks and not succeeding, but proud of how quickly she'd picked it up, Natalie relaxed. She had done that without too much difficulty. How much worse could this be?

She tried not to think about it too hard and did her best to hold it steady and activate the magic. The train jolted and she lost the spot again. She found it again and tried the next bit, but still nothing happened.

"I'm not sure I can do this," she told the werewolf when she had the same problem a third time.

"You're almost there. One more try and I'm sure you'll have it."

The encouragement and jovial tone from Francisco was enough to steady Natalie again. She brought the device back where it needed to be, this time waiting until she was very sure. She concentrated on the same feeling she'd had when she'd used magic in the cemetery.

After a strange hum for a couple of seconds, the light went out on the triangle.

"I think I did it," she exclaimed.

Francisco turned and took the triangle from her.

"Well, I think you probably did, but either way we must continue. This is now out of juice, so to speak."

Natalie nodded, but some of the pressure and fear returned at his admission. If it wasn't working, they had no way of knowing whether it had succeeded or not without the glasses to detect it. And Rich had the glasses.

Before she could point this out or make something else happen, Francisco grabbed her arm and hurried her out of the bathroom as the train began to slow and pull into a station. Although they had tickets to go further, they were getting off here.

"Now. Our friends need us." The werewolf grinned as they got off at the stop and he hurried Natalie along with him.

Within minutes, the charming creature had persuaded a local taxi driver to take them to catch the other train. It was an ambitious goal, but a fun prospect.

"Aren't you worried that he'll talk about us and recognize us because we've been too memorable?

"Nonsense," Francisco assured her. "I'll make him forget us. He'll have loads of money and be happy and we'll be forgotten entirely."

Trying not to worry about Natalie, Rich settled into the train seat opposite Alia. Getting separated wasn't part of the plan, but Natalie had shot him a message telling him not to panic, that Francisco had a plan of some kind and they'd be together soon.

"They'll get to us," Alia assured Rich.

The three of them traveled in silence for several stops. Rich was grateful that no conductor came down to check their tickets, as Natalie had them. They also had no way of hiding Lucas.

Somehow, their luck held and they pulled up to a sleepy

village station. Alia spotted Natalie and Francisco running for the platform.

All three of them cheered when the pair made it in time to slip through the doors, despite drawing looks from the other passengers.

It didn't take long for everyone to fill each other in on everything that had happened, and Rich was able to confirm that Natalie had succeeded in deactivating the tracker the enforcers had put on the werewolf.

Now they were all back together, Francisco took over and got them to their next destination, which he'd worked out along the way. He's been reading the book he had taken and somehow materialized it again. Whatever magic he had, he seemed to have the equivalent of a Mary Poppins bag somewhere.

They pulled into another nearby town, where they needed to get a taxi a few miles out into the country. The driver spoke enough English that Rich and Francisco managed to persuade him to hand over a phone number so that they could get a ride back to town when they were done.

As the driver pulled away, they turned and looked around. They were in the foothills of a small mountain range in the middle of nowhere. There were a few trees around, but it was mostly grassland.

Francisco led them forward and through the hills.

"Have we forgotten something?" Natalie asked when they had gone about half a mile away from the road. Rich had begun having the same feeling, but when Alia and Francisco both laughed, he was glad he wasn't the one who had voiced it.

"This area is sort of protected. It makes you want to go home or think you left the oven on, or something like that," Alia explained.

"It means we are finally close." Francisco sounded serious for a moment and had a strange light in his eyes. Unlike the sadness he'd had at the mansion, however, this was a proud light. Whatever they were coming toward, it was important to the werewolf.

He stopped at the entrance to what looked like a small cave in one of the smaller mounds of the foothills. Old, gnarled trees stood on either side of the opening like sentries.

"Is this it?" Alia asked. "*This* is the big were library?"

"Alia!" Rich exclaimed.

"It's okay," Francisco assured them both. "It's a lot more impressive than it looks. Inside."

No one said what all of them were thinking: this had better be good inside, or they had come a long way for nothing.

Francisco took the first step forward, but Alia put her hand out.

"Movement." She nodded toward the cave entrance.

Less than a second after she spoke, what looked like a statue came walking out of the cave entrance. It was shaped like an upright werewolf in its true form and lumbered along. Another followed that, then another, and all three formed a row in front of the entrance.

Natalie picked up Lucas before anything could happen to him, and murmured, "This doesn't look good."

CHAPTER THIRTY-ONE

The three statues in front of the cave didn't move at first, and Alia wondered if they were going to do anything but stand there. The message was plenty clear, though. There would be no getting into this cave without facing these creatures. It wasn't a pleasant thought. Of everything they had done to get here, so far they hadn't had to fight anything that could kill them.

Francisco nodded at each of them in turn. "Well, my friends, I would understand if none of you wanted to go any further. This is not the most welcome sight, and you have already done so much for me."

"Even if we didn't need the possible cure in there for Lucas, we'd be helping you now," Rich replied, though he gulped as he surveyed the moving statues. "At least, as much as that's possible anyway."

"We've got this." Natalie helped Lucas up onto her shoulders. She sounded confident, but Alia thought that was fear in the woman's eyes. Who wouldn't be scared?

Alia pulled out the stone bending device, hoping it

would work on these things. Francisco set down his luggage and transformed himself. It didn't take long before he was the spitting, living image of the statues ahead, and Alia didn't doubt that he was every bit as deadly.

That meant one of the statues was going to be taken care of, but there were two more. Even if she could handle one of them by herself with her device, that left one more for Rich, Natalie, and Lucas.

Francisco pulled out the second device, turned it on, and threw it toward Natalie. This seemed to be enough of a trigger that the statues began to move, taking a step toward the group and then another until they were almost running.

The werewolf on their side did the same, and headed straight for the middle statue. They clashed, snarling, and whirled around each other, dodging blows and swipes and sending them back in turn.

Alia attacked the one nearest her and hit its shoulder with the rock melding device. It screamed and spun to face her. She ducked a retaliation swipe and tried to get into a position to hit it again. It kept coming at her, forcing her to retreat over the uneven ground and weave back and forth. A few seconds later, she realized it had divided her from the group.

It gave her a view to the other side of Francisco, where Natalie had managed to get herself up onto a fallen tree on the rise in the hill and was trying to blast the closest statue to her. It wasn't working, but Rich came to her rescue, throwing rocks, sticks, dirt, and whatever he could get his hands on.

The three groups continued to shuffle, the statues

giving no ground and seemingly impervious to everything thrown at them.

Alia dodged another swipe but wasn't fast enough, and the stone paw clipped her side, sending her reeling. Pain flared and she grunted and took a few steps, then she tripped over something and went down.

More pain radiated from her elbow and back, but she rolled as the statue tried to smash down with a fist and crush her. She rolled again as it bellowed, but then a chunk of rock hit it on the side of the head.

"Over here, you oversized garden decoration," Natalie yelled. She ran around the top of the hill above the cave entrance and threw another stone, using the hand device and magic as well as her own brute strength. The statue attacking Alia paused to look Natalie's way, which gave the elf time to scramble back to her feet.

As soon as she was upright again, she raised her device and aimed it at the statue's leg. She deformed it and pushed the leg into an unnatural position that made it wobble.

Natalie hurled a second rock. It missed the statue, but it lurched to one side as it continued to cry out in pain, and its leg was so mangled that it fell over. Natalie squealed in delight and pumped her fist in the air.

The statue crashed into a tree, and a crack appeared along the shoulder and down the arm before it bounced sideways. As it hit the ground, the other arm broke off. Alia redirected her magical device and aimed at the only fully working limb. Instead of just mangling it this time, she forced it down into the ground and connected it to the stone that the hill was made of under the dirt and loam.

This seemed to be too much for the magical attacker. It split down the middle and went still.

"A little help over here!" Rich shouted as Natalie cheered again.

Alia turned that way in time to see the statue try to hit him at the same time as he tried to swing a large tree branch at it. The statue's arm hit the branch and shattered it. Bits of wood and splinters went flying. Rich ducked, throwing his arms up to protect his face.

The statue was about to hit him again when Lucas jumped from a tree and landed on its head. The cat covered the creature's eyes for a moment and made it wobble. It gave Rich a moment to collect himself and step back, and Alia ran around Francisco and his sparring counterpart.

With the cat on its head and Natalie also hurling things and starting to get more of a sense of control of the magical device again, the animated defender bellowed and screeched and flailed.

Several times, Alia had to duck, and Lucas slid around. His claws couldn't gain purchase on the stone, so he jumped clear before a stone hand almost knocked him off.

The cat had done what he needed to, however, and Natalie and Alia both got close enough to start bending the stone while Rich grabbed Lucas and got him out of harm's way. As Alia grabbed control of a hand and bent it around, Natalie hurled another sharp-looking rock.

At the moment the statue whirled to attack Alia, the large stone hit and put a crack across the statue's back. It bellowed as if it truly felt the pain and spun again.

Alia took the opening to attack again. She focused once

more and tried to root the statue's leg to the rock underneath as she had the first. It either didn't connect with anything, or the statue was strong enough still to break free.

Before she could lock it in place and see if it broke like the last one, it lurched toward Alia and struck out at her. It seemed to have worked out that she was the worst threat.

"Hey, you brainless hunk of badly carved art," Rich yelled. He picked up the largest piece of the tree branch that had shattered and hurled it at the statue. Although it struck it in the face, whatever intelligence the animated stone had gave it enough sense to ignore this and keep swinging at Alia.

Ducking and rolling to one side, Alia tried to stay ahead of its moves. For something made of stone, it moved quickly. It was faster than the other statue had been, as if this one was somehow stronger.

Alia focused on moving fast and hoped that Natalie, Rich, and Lucas could come up with a way to defeat it before it outwitted her.

She was unable to see Francisco anymore, but she occasionally heard a bellow or grunt from his direction, from both the living and the stone werewolf. It let her know that their werewolf friend was still alive. She hoped that was enough for now.

With Rich hurling insults and whatever he could lay his hands on, Lucas trying to climb a nearby tree to launch from again, and Natalie doing her best with the other stone manipulator, Alia had all the help she could want. She couldn't find an opening, though. Each limb that came her way moved so fast that she could do little more than lead it around in circles and keep it busy. It wasn't sustainable, but she continued to look for some way of hurting it.

Before she could find that opening, Francisco roared triumphantly, followed by the sound of stone cracking.

For a fraction of a second, the statue in front of Alia stopped, as if hesitating now that it stood alone. Then it renewed its attack, and Alia had to throw herself to the ground to avoid the fastest swing yet. It swung at her, trying to slam its fist down on her prone body. She rolled, but she was no longer fast enough.

Francisco managed to block the attack a few inches from her face, using the limb from the other statue. There was a loud sharp sound, but both stones held and Alia rolled away as Francisco stepped into the fray.

He was already panting, blood dripping from various wounds, but he had a determined look in his eyes.

"They get faster with each one that we defeat," he explained as he used the broken statue arm like a sword, attacking and parrying several more times.

Alia took a few seconds to survey the remaining threat. He was right. And it made sense, given the magic that must have been powering them. It made a more effective line of defense, and if it had a set amount of reserve power from somewhere in the cave, all of it was now being fed into the one statue.

This was going to need all of them.

Though they were all exhausted, Rich and Natalie grew more furious and frantic in their attacks as well, dancing around the statue as it focused on the living werewolf. Alia waded back in, and lifted the device once more, aiming carefully.

It was harder to get a clear angle now that it moved so much faster and was hitting with more force. On top of that, Francisco was dancing it around more than Alia had —his style of fighting was more like that of a knight or old swordsman.

She took every opportunity she could to morph small sections of the statue and hurt it enough to distract it from the werewolf. Francisco made the most of every opportunity the others gave him and smacked the creature hard with the limb of its fallen comrade. It was teamwork in motion, and every little strike and attack was wearing it down.

Before long, the statue had so many cracks and missing fragments that it had gone from looking almost brand new to looking as if it had stood out in the weather for a thousand years.

It was finally beginning to slow, lurching awkwardly from a knee joint that didn't work the way it had.

"I cannot keep this up much longer," Francisco warned them between pants for air.

A moment later, the piece of statue he'd been wielding shattered and the pieces flew everywhere, making all of them but the statue duck.

The werewolf fell back but the statue didn't stop. For every step Francisco took, it advanced.

Alia and Natalie came together, and the elf pointed to each of the legs. It was now or never. The werewolf tripped and stumbled, and Lucas chose his moment to jump onto its head.

It roared and tried to remove the cat. Francisco scrambled back as Rich stepped forward, swinging another stone limb. At the same time, Alia and Natalie came close enough and focused on the statue's feet.

Putting everything she had into the magical device in her hand, Alia succeeded in rooting a foot to the bedrock underneath and noticed that Natalie was managing to do the same.

The statue cried out, still trying to pull Lucas off. Now that the stone was chipped and cracked, the cat could more easily move about and get his claws into the statue to evade the groping hands. Several fingers were now gone, which made the task even easier.

Given time to recover and with Alia and Natalie having pinned the statue in one place, Francisco took the second stone limb from Rich.

He waited for the right moment and then struck.

The statue had one of its own limbs, and Lucas clung to the other while he tried to get back to the head. He needn't have bothered. The statue went still and cracked down the center.

For a moment no one moved. They were all panting hard, exhausted, and hurting.

Alia and Francisco had fared the worst in terms of injuries, but they were also the two who had magic to help them and would heal the most swiftly.

"Thank you, my friends. I could not have done that without your aid, and I hope that none of you are harmed," Francisco finally said.

"Some bruises, but I'll live," Alia replied. She held up the magic stone device to show that it was burned out. It had cracked as well.

The other one was intact, and Natalie handed it to Francisco and let him deactivate it.

"Let us hope that is the last of them." The werewolf stepped over a broken statue part and toward the cave entrance.

CHAPTER THIRTY-TWO

Natalie's mouth fell open as they rounded the corner in the cave. Lights had been coming on magically for the were-wolf as he stepped deeper, and there hadn't been any more nasty surprises in terms of defenses, but nothing could have prepared her for the Unplace that lay before them.

It was by far the biggest library known to the world, but it was also more than a library. There were cabinets of items, display cases, and mannequins sporting all sorts of clothing.

Time and decay had impacted some of it, a jacket so moth eaten and rotted that it was growing mold and hung off the wire frame torso it had been placed on. The glass on some of the display cases was also cracked, but every single book appeared to be perfectly preserved as far as Natalie could tell.

She moved toward the nearest one, but Alia stopped her.

"There's a lot of magic in here. And if those statues

were the only deterrent, then I'm going to be very surprised," she explained.

"Alia is correct," Francisco added. "There will be several curses. On the bookshelves, but also on displays and areas of the floor. We must move carefully and stay together. I would not want to see one of you harmed now when we are so close to finding what we need."

Natalie scooped up Lucas again, wanting to make sure that he didn't wander off. He'd begun to struggle to focus. It worried her, but hopefully it wouldn't be much longer now.

"Where first?" Alia asked. "Do you know where we need to go?"

"I have an inkling that what we need will be deeper, but I can't be sure. There's a specific route through, however. And given the challenges we've already faced, I think we should do our best to follow it."

Natalie had no intention of making a fuss about that either. This was not something she could help with. She felt tired enough from trying to use the last magic item and fighting with it.

Looking around and taking steps in random directions, Francisco absorbed himself in the task of figuring out their direction while the others stood around.

Francisco decided they should head to their left, away from the majority of the books and toward what looked like a dead end.

Rich hesitated. "Are you sure?"

"You want to go a different way, feel free to try it. But I'm only going to help break so many curses on you three before I give up and go back to the US," Francisco informed him.

"Noted," Rich replied, coming in closer and following. Natalie stifled a grin and waited for their companions to figure out the next step. She wanted to help, but she had no idea where to begin.

Alia stepped up beside Francisco and tilted her head to the side as if she was listening. She pointed at something to one side near the ground and Francisco nodded.

"Well spotted, *ma chère*. I had a feeling you would be good at this."

"You held your ground with those statues, the least I can do is help with these curses."

Natalie watched as Alia stepped a little closer to a box on the floor. Crouching, she pulled a small tool from her boot. It looked a bit like an elongated spoon, but below the bowl of it was a very small hook.

It also had a tapered handle, which Alia seemed to find useful for using the tool in a very fine motion. She reached out with it and muttered some words. It began to glow, and as it came close to the box, it met something that flashed and radiated outwards like a forcefield of some kind.

Pausing there, Alia continued to mutter to herself until light flashes traveled across the surface of the orange forcefield, heading toward the strange hooked spoon and then into it and up the shaft.

This carried on for several minutes, the pulses getting faster as something appeared to gain momentum until it slowed again. The orange had almost entirely faded. As suddenly as it appeared, the forcefield blinked out.

"Wonderful work," Francisco exclaimed as he walked forward.

Natalie tucked herself in behind the werewolf, giving him enough space that she didn't look as if she was using him for protection. She noticed Rich doing the same with Alia.

They passed the nearest bookshelves and scanned the titles, but as interesting as they were, none of them were the books or artifacts they were looking for.

It also wasn't long before they reached the next section to revive after a long time preserved under a curse. This time Francisco spotted a trip wire that led to a strange trinket that would have been triggered.

Once again, Alia pulled the tool from her boot and got to work. This time, there didn't seem to be anything magical involved in the trap itself, but Natalie had no doubt that wherever the trip wire led would shoot something nasty.

After ushering everyone back, Alia got down on her knees and followed the wire across, trying to find the best place to disarm it.

"This is complicated," she told them when she had found the section of cave wall where the right side entered. "I can try and disarm this one, but there's a chance that it's going to go off anyway."

"Do what you can," Francisco urged her, and motioned for all of them but the elf to take another few steps back.

She rolled her eyes at their fear and picked a spot to cut the wire. The tool had a clamp on either side of some very fine and sharp-looking clippers. Alia put them on and held the wire steady.

Natalie barely dared to breathe as she watched Alia get everything in position and cut the wire. With the clamps holding it, the whole thing stayed where it was. Alia then let the left clamp go, taking the strain of the wire herself and holding it in place. She eased it off to the right.

The sound of a large crack came a second later.

"Get back," she yelled, and threw herself backward as well. Green gas started to vent out of the side of the wall in several different places.

They all ran backward a few paces as Francisco fumbled with something in the strange Unplace pocket he had. A few seconds later he pulled out a small flat box and tapped a few buttons on the side to open it.

He skidded it across the floor toward the gas. The box sucked in air and made a strange whirring noise, and as Natalie watched, the green vapor was pulled inside it.

The trap ran out of puff a minute in, but it had pumped out so much so quickly that a lot was in the air and it took the box several more minutes to suck it all up and clear the air.

Francisco made them wait a few more minutes, and eventually the box seemed to decide it was done of its own accord. It stopped sucking air in and closed back up again.

It beeped a few times as the werewolf moved forward.

"Let us hope we do not encounter another trap like that," he muttered and stuffed it back into his Unplace pouch.

In the next section, a couple of books interested Alia. They were both about something Natalie didn't understand. Francisco found a strange wristband on one of the shelves and tucked it into his pouch without explanation.

Natalie thought she could feel something growing as they moved deeper and disarmed more curses and traps along the way.

They wound their way around the library, finding some very useful objects and managing to avoid setting off anything else for now. They left a lot of the things they found, like a jacket that made the wearer smell nice, or a pocket watch that could speed up the growth of flowers. Francisco seemed to take great delight in explaining everything to them. He recognized many of the artifacts by sight and knew what to expect from a lot of the rest of the library.

They got closer to the back where the books were kept behind display cabinets with traps and curses on them. Now none of them dared touch anything they weren't here for. Natalie felt as if she were in Aladdin's cave, where she wasn't meant to touch anything but the fancy gemstone that the bad guy wanted.

Except the bad guy who wanted it had come in with them and risked his life and helped them get it. And he wasn't a bad guy.

They didn't have to go much further before Francisco threw his hands up in the air in delight.

"Here it is. The book we need to help your friend. I knew it would be in here somewhere." Francisco didn't explain any more than that but inspected the display case as Alia stepped up to do the same.

"This isn't going to be easy to open," she told him a few seconds later. "And even if we did open it, there's a pressure plate and motion sensor inside."

Francisco sighed and stepped back. The pair of them

conferred in hushed whispers for a few minutes, pointing out elements of the display case. Natalie tried to pay attention, but she couldn't make out everything that they said.

Alia pulled out one final tool, this time from a pouch on her back that had remained hidden under her jacket the entire time.

It was a glass-cutting device that looked sharp and clever, and it reminded Natalie that Alia was a thief and had practiced these sorts of things. If anyone could get this book without setting off a trap, it was the elf.

"Right. You all might want to get back from the case as I do this," Alia cautioned. Francisco didn't leave her side.

"This will be easier with two," he offered. "I can help."

For a moment Natalie thought Alia might argue, but then she moved over so he could reach everything beside her. She placed the cutter on the glass and paused to take several deep breaths.

Working slowly, she ran what looked a bit like an old-fashioned school compass around in a circle large enough that the book would fit through.

Once she'd done a single rotation, Natalie expected her to stop and pull out the circle of glass, but she moved the cutter around again and again. The concentration on Alia's face as she kept glancing to one side made Natalie wonder what other factor was influencing this behavior.

Alia paused and focused in front of her again.

"I think this is cut through now."

"Marvelous. You have a steady hand and an eye for these things. You must have made it very difficult on the enforcers in your home area."

Alia grinned at Francisco's praise. She focused again

and tried to gently pull out the glass panel. It didn't give, so she circled the cutter once more. This time when she pulled, the glass section slid out, showing itself to be almost a centimeter thick.

As she pulled the device off the glass, Francisco lifted one of the books he had picked up earlier. It was about the same size and weight as the book they were going to take.

Natalie held her breath as Francisco eased the book through the gap, making sure he didn't touch the glass as he did. Once it was inside, he held it above the other book, and Alia pulled out one final tool. It looked a bit like a long, thin spatula with a digital display on the handle.

She slipped the device under the book, between it and the pressure plate. It gave her a reading and she nodded at the werewolf. While she held the tool steady and kept the digital display reading the same number, Francisco held up the first book they wanted and pulled it outwards.

As soon as it was out of the slot, he lowered the replacement book until it sat on top of the tool and took its place.

"It's too light," Alia reported a second later.

No one moved, and the werewolf frowned.

"We need about another quarter of a pound." Alia exhaled and looked up at Francisco. He still had both hands in the display case with the book in there, and while Alia was holding the tool against the pressure plate, he couldn't pull it out. Neither of them could move.

Natalie looked around for something that might work. She hurried back toward the opening and gathered up some rocks from outside. She brought a whole bunch of different sizes and held them out to Francisco.

He added more of them to the top of the book, waiting

each time for Alia to adjust the tool and make sure the pressure stayed as consistent as possible.

Before long, it was equal to before. The pressure plate tool let Alia know it was equivalent with a very happy sounding beep.

Everyone exhaled with relief.

Alia went first, easing out her tool while Francisco stood there with the book, holding as still as he could. As soon as she stepped back, her part of the job done, he shifted to the center and pulled the book through the opening. It was easier bringing it out, but the werewolf was still cautious and took his time.

When he was done, the grin that spread across his face was well earned. As they all stepped back, the book they needed finally in their possession, Natalie exhaled. Hopefully now they would be able to get their friend back.

Francisco flipped through the pages, the only one of the group who could read the book. The concentration on his face was too much for Natalie to bear. She looked away, toward the entrance of the cave. She saw movement.

"Company," she gritted out. They dove behind the nearest bookcase and out of sight. Alia used a mirror to peek backward and confirm that several enforcers had come into the cave.

"We cannot let them take anything from here," Francisco whispered as he half-closed the book. "I must turn myself in again to distract them."

"Are you sure?" Natalie asked, feeling as if she might cry again. This felt so unfair after all he had been doing for them.

"I am positive. It must be done. We must present a front that keeps you all safe."

"But there's no way that we'll be able to try the same tricks to rescue you."

"No, you shouldn't attempt it this time." Francisco nodded to Alia, who already held handcuffs out for him. While Natalie was set against it, she knew there would be no arguing.

Once again, Alia took the werewolf to the enforcers in handcuffs.

"Don't let him get away this time." She sounded as exhausted as Natalie felt.

It was over. Right at the last minute, they were going to have to give up.

CHAPTER THIRTY-THREE

Rich watched the mass of enforcers gather around the cave entrance and frowned.

"I wouldn't go in there if I were you," Alia called to them. "We didn't disarm all the traps and cursed areas, just what we needed to in order to catch the werewolf. It's hostile to anyone not of that race and there's nothing important in there really. Just a bunch of books on magic that barely works and pathetic treasures of a race no longer powerful."

Although Alia's words sounded as if they were dripping with disdain, Rich knew better now. There had been a lot in there that was important. Not least, the possible cure for Lucas.

Now the enforcers had Francisco, and Alia had already warned her friends that there were more powerful enforcers here than there had been the last time. None of them understood how they had gotten here so fast, or even managed to find them, but they had and they had already carted Francisco off toward the road.

"So, about that reward," Alia mentioned to the nearest detective.

"Yes, I believe you were promised one, and since you've delivered him to us not once, but twice, it's only fair that I sign over the payment to you." The detective smiled as Natalie looked at Rich.

While Alia handed over bank details and organized the logistics of the three of them getting paid for their part in capturing Francisco, Natalie leaned closer to Rich.

"I'm not sure we should take this," she whispered. "We haven't captured him. We've helped him escape and we all know that we'd do it again."

"I know what you mean," Rich replied.

The two of them looked at each other, and Rich opened his mouth to say something before Lucas hissed at him from a few feet away.

Raising his eyebrows, Rich looked at the cat and tried to work out what must have upset him. The detective had everything he needed and was walking away as Rich held out his hand toward Lucas to encourage the cat forward.

"What is it, buddy?" Rich asked, but Lucas lifted his head and strode toward Alia.

"If I'm stuck as a cat a little longer, then there's no way you're turning down my cut of the reward money. They asked us to help find Francisco. We found him and he went to them willingly."

"The cat has a point," Alia put in. "We've been doing as they asked, and there's not much we can do about it now. We might as well take the reward money and get something good out of it."

Sighing, Rich nodded. "Okay. We'll take it. But I still feel guilty. This isn't what we intended to do at all. And we broke him out once."

"No one came to any harm, and they got him back," Natalie pointed out. A moment later she tilted her head to the side. "I feel bad that we've had to hand him over again and we still don't know how to help Lucas."

"I'm sure we could find someone who speaks were," Alia replied. "Admittedly, it might take a while to find someone who not only understands it but who we can be sure won't screw us over."

Lucas sighed loudly and let Rich pick him up.

"We'll find a way to get you back, buddy. I swear." Rich gave him head scritches and hoped it wouldn't be too late.

"I want to talk to him," Natalie added without a pause.

Rich looked at her as if she had gone crazy. What did she mean? Who?

"I need to talk to him."

"Are you sure?" Alia asked. "He's not going to help us now and chances are that the enforcers aren't going to leave you alone with him. You know that, right?"

"It's worth a try. And I don't want him to think that we betrayed him." Natalie stalked toward the small area of the hillside where the enforcers were holding the werewolf while they waited for a secure vehicle and more backup to take the werewolf away. After he'd escaped from the nearest prison, they didn't appear to be taking any more chances.

Rich handed Lucas to Alia and went with her.

"I'd like to talk to Francisco alone, please," Natalie requested as soon as they reached the enforcer near him.

"I've got some questions to ask him about a trap he set and it's important."

"I'm not sure we can leave you alone with him. He's escaped once already," the enforcer replied in a thick accent.

Rich was grateful that this wasn't the set of enforcers from the prison earlier. They were likely to be suspicious if they saw Natalie there again.

"I know it's going to go against protocol, but we helped you capture this guy not once but twice. And we're not about to let him go so we have to catch him a third time."

The enforcer paused and set his jaw for a moment. Rich was sure he was about to say no, but instead he nodded.

"Okay. You have earned it."

If only he knew, Rich thought.

Natalie thanked him and walked closer to where they were keeping the werewolf.

There was another enforcer in front of the entrance, but the guy was waved off by the one she'd just spoken to. He looked suspiciously at Natalie and Rich but didn't stop them as they went inside.

Francisco grinned when he saw them, and Rich instantly felt a little better.

"I'm so sorry," Natalie began before he could speak. "I swear we had no idea they would find us."

"Oh, hush, please, *ma chère*. I know this was not your doing, not after the lengths that you and your friends went to in getting me out the last time and helping me get here." Francisco focused on Natalie and Rich frowned. He felt as if he wasn't wanted and he didn't like it.

"Is there anything we can—"

Francisco held up his hand and stopped Natalie's offer.

"There is nothing you can do this time. If you were to aid me again, you would make it far more obvious that you were helping me. Once is enough. I will be fine. I thank you for thinking of me, but I must go with these good few and see what is to be done about these fake charges. I will soon know if there is any chance of having them dropped. They cannot have much in the way of evidence."

Rich felt a little better hearing this. The thought of worrying any more about doing the wrong thing and being discovered by the enforcers had gotten to him.

Natalie moved forward and hugged the werewolf.

"Thank you for trying to help us. It means a lot that you went through so much to help."

"Ah, *ma chère*, on that score, do not be disappointed. I know that you did everything you could to help me, and I have had a little time to finish upholding my end of our little deal."

"You have?" Natalie stepped back, her eyes wide.

The smile on Francisco's face grew. "When you get out of here and find yourself alone somewhere, take a look in your back pocket."

Natalie paused as if about to ask what he meant, but the enforcers came back before she could.

"We must take him now. I hope you have said what you need."

"Yes, thank you," Rich replied for Natalie.

Although Natalie shot him a look to suggest that she was *not* done, he beelined for the exit and hoped that she was following. She was.

Neither of them spoke until they were back with Alia a little way away from everyone else.

"Any idea where they're going to take him?" Alia asked as they all watched Francisco being escorted to a car with several new enforcers. "Those guys have some powerful magic auras coming off them."

"He didn't say but he told us he understood that it wasn't us. No hard feelings," Rich explained.

Natalie reached into her back pocket as Francisco had suggested, and her eyes went wide as she pulled out a folded piece of paper.

"Are you kidding me?" She stared at the thing in her palm.

"Looks like he was telling the truth about that too." Rich chuckled as Natalie continued to stare at it, confused.

"How did he do that? He must have groped my ass to slip it in and I didn't even notice I was getting felt up. How is that even possible?"

It was Alia's turn to laugh. "He's sneaky all right. What does it say?"

Natalie unfolded it and took a look. "It's coordinates. For a GPS device. And instructions for a ritual. Something that looks pretty simple. We're going to need some wildflowers and a few supplies, but nothing a shop in town wouldn't sell us."

"Okay. So we have another place to go." Rich took Lucas back from Alia and the group turned to go back to the enforcers. They were going to need to get a lift back to the town if they were going to make good time, but Rich reckoned he could persuade the enforcers to help them out with that as well.

CHAPTER THIRTY-FOUR

A mountain loomed before them in the early morning light. It had taken them most of the evening before to get to the nearest town and then a hike this morning to get them closer to the coordinates. Now they had a climb, but the GPS was telling them that they were close.

Natalie felt as if it was a bit like treasure hunting. They knew they were close to the place they needed. It was easy to think of this as a fun outing, but she carried Lucas in her arms, and he had barely said a sentence all morning. This was probably his last chance.

They climbed up a winding path that looked as if someone had carved it into the mountain a long time ago. Natalie noticed a way marker by the side of the path, a strange stone with different markings on it.

"Do you know what these mean?" Rich asked Alia.

"They're counting down to something in were."

"Counting down to what?" Natalie pressed. A chill ran through her. It was getting colder as they climbed, and it was eerily quiet.

"I guess we're going to find out, because the GPS is pointing in the same direction and seems to be following the same rough decrease." Alia frowned, holding the device.

They continued for several more minutes. The silence grew worse and the path grew wider but steeper. As they went up the next section, Natalie spotted several stakes. Each one sported bones of different sizes and sections of fur. It looked like a macabre warning for people not to go any further.

Alia reassured them that they were safe so far. There wasn't the feel of magic ahead of them.

When the stakes started to get closer together and more was hanging from them, Alia slowed.

"This is leading to something that I don't want to disrespect. You've been invited by Francisco, and he gave you the coordinates, but I'm an elf and given what I've learned the last week or so, I don't want to upset anyone or do anything inappropriate."

Natalie guessed Rich would have argued if Alia had given him the chance. Instead, without looking back, she strutted off, heading back down the mountain path.

Rich hesitated, but Natalie encouraged him to keep going. She held the cat to her chest and flicked her head in his direction. They needed to carry on and see this through, even if it was dangerous.

There were a couple more turns before the path reached a plateau on the side of the mountain. It wasn't a large area, but it was clearly something with purpose. A circle made with bleached white bones was in the center of more stakes and furs. Someone had also put up leather cuttings between the stakes to act as windbreaks across the area.

Natalie pulled out the piece of paper Francisco had given her and followed the beginning part of the instructions as best as she could. She placed Lucas in the middle of the circle and added all the other items they'd been told to gather.

"Do you think this will work?" Natalie asked Rich when they had everything almost ready and the nerves were getting to her.

"I'm more worried about whether we're alone," he replied in a low whisper while nodding as if everything was okay.

Natalie didn't respond. If someone was watching, it could be bad. They might stop them part way through the ritual or do something even worse. But if someone was happy to just watch them, maybe the best thing was to ignore them.

Seeming to have already decided how to handle everything, Rich continued to prepare the ritual Francisco had laid out for them and then read through the details again.

"Okay. I think we're ready." Rich gave Lucas one last head scritch before he stepped back and out of the circle.

He and Natalie then took deep breaths and began to chant as instructed. It wasn't an activity that Natalie was particularly comfortable with, but she did her best to do what Francisco had asked for and she put her heart into it. Lucas needed her to.

For a few seconds, Lucas sat in the middle of the circle, a little bemused by the whole thing. It appeared as if he didn't understand it, and he got up as if he wanted to leave the circle.

Before he could wander out of the circle and ruin everything, the bones glowed faintly and the items piled up around Lucas began to smoke as if burning without any actual fire there.

Lucas yowled as if he was in pain, and Natalie automatically shifted to go to him. Rich managed to stop her before she crossed the line of bones and screwed up the ritual herself.

Terrified she'd do more harm than good, Natalie carried on chanting and following the instructions. While they spoke the words they had been given, Natalie sprinkled herbs and flowers around the circle and chucked them toward the circle.

All of it burned up as if it was on fire, though there wasn't any. Everything burned except for Lucas. He remained sitting in the middle.

When they finished the full set of instructions and they had chanted for as long as directed, they stopped and looked at their friend. He was still a cat, and all that had happened was that their ingredients were gone and the bones had lit up with a magic glow.

Natalie stood stock still, trying not to cry. What did they do now?

After a few moments, Rich went to step over the line as well, but suddenly Lucas was glowing, faintly at first, then brighter. He rose into the air and began to spin. When the spinning slowed, they saw he was beginning to change shape and find his feet again.

Natalie realized that he was coming back to them naked

when skin started to emerge where fur had been. She turned away, her cheeks flushing, as much in empathy for Lucas as embarrassment for herself.

"Shit, this is cold," Lucas complained a moment later.

Rich scrambled to get clothes for Lucas to wear back down the mountain, but he had nothing with him unless he wanted to strip.

"There's a blanket in Alia's kit and I happen to be carrying some of it." Natalie realized Rich didn't have anything that would fit their friend.

It took her a while to rummage, and all the while she could hear Lucas behind her shivering. She got him wrapped up and they all agreed that they needed to get back to the hotel.

As he tried to walk, he stumbled.

"I don't think I work quite right anymore," Lucas muttered. His gait was off and he didn't seem to be able to multitask properly and concentrate on walking.

"You'll get used to it again." Natalia hoped that was true and that she hadn't been misled. Hopefully he would come back to them. It was a good sign that he was talking, and she encouraged him to keep doing so while they walked. Rich supported Lucas physically and helped keep the blanket around him.

"This is cold." Lucas repeated, sounding forlorn and not happy that they'd turned him back the way they had.

"Sorry. We'll get you some more clothes as soon as we're back at the hotel. Let's get you down the mountain. It's not far." Natalie was mostly lying, but it was the best she could do right now.

Natalie did her best to concentrate on talking to Lucas

about inane things, but the subject kept coming back to life as a cat for the last few weeks and how difficult that had been. It was one of the worst times of Lucas's life, but he had learned a lot.

When they got back to where Alia was, the elf was sitting partway down the path and staring off at the horizon. She smiled when she saw them, and then she took in the blanket and lack of clothes.

"That's an issue I didn't expect, but I'm glad you're back to yourself," Alia called to them as they got closer.

By the time they'd got to her, the sun had come out from behind a cloud and helped to warm Lucas. Alia was also far stronger than she looked, and she swapped places with Natalie to support him. Within seconds, she was making it look easy.

They got a few weird looks when they returned to the town nearby, but they were supporting a guy wrapped in a blanket who didn't appear to be able to walk very well. People got out of their way and seemed to assume that he was injured and being aided.

A few noticed that Alia was a lot stronger than she appeared to be and this puzzled them, but it wasn't as if Natalie could tell them that she was an elf as if it explained everything. No one would believe them anyway. But none of that mattered. They had their friend back.

CHAPTER THIRTY-FIVE

Natalie came down to breakfast back in Alia's Unplace, grateful to be back to normal to some degree. She smiled.

"Not like that," Rich exclaimed when Lucas almost dropped his cereal bowl. He still held the spoon in a strange way and instinctively went to lap up the contents from it rather than put it in his mouth.

Natalie grinned at Rich as she went to get herself breakfast.

Lucas had been human again for three days, but his time as a cat had made an impact. Already he was returning to himself, but there were a few habits that might take a little while to break. As if to make her point without even knowing it, Lucas sat and rubbed at his face with the side of his hand before licking it.

Rich and Natalie both burst out laughing.

"What did he do this time?" Alia yelled from upstairs. "Was I right?"

"You were right," Rich called back. "He went to clean himself with his hands."

"I think you guys should try being stuck as a cat for several weeks and see how you adjust. It's weird and I don't think I should be blamed for it."

"Oh, we're not blaming you. You're being very entertaining. I think you can take pride in how you're providing us all with so much amusement." Natalie gave him a cheeky grin as Alia came down the stairs.

The elf had her phone in her hand and plodded down as if she wasn't paying attention. It was such a marked change in expression to just a few seconds earlier that it was clear something had happened.

"What's wrong?" Rich asked, beating Natalie to it.

"I've got a message from the enforcers in France. They've sent the reward money as promised, but Francisco has broken out of prison again. He managed to persuade one of the wardens overnight to bring him an extra blanket because he was cold. They let their guard down just a little bit too much and with some magic item he got himself out again."

"He really is incredibly charming, isn't he?" Rich sighed almost wistfully, as if he hoped to one day be as persuasive and disarm people so well.

Natalie didn't respond. It was good to have more money. They would be able to pay off the last of the credit card debt and still have enough left over that they could live on it a while. It was nice to be back in the green and not feel the pressure.

It was also good to have Lucas back, even if he was still adjusting. He was returning, and that was good enough.

None of that compared to the thrill of delight she felt on hearing that Francisco was free once more. Seeing him give himself up to protect them a second time had won her over and it had pained her to think he was going to face a fake charge.

Him being free made her happy in a way she hadn't expected to feel.

She imagined what he might be doing. Whether he would go back to the library, or if he would try something else next, or maybe even consider himself done and retire.

She got a text message and her phone vibrated against her leg. She unlocked it and pulled down the notification.

Her mouth almost fell open when she saw that it was from the werewolf himself and he was asking her if she wanted to go out on a date when he was next in the US.

The shock turned into a grin as she hurried away to her room.

"I'm just going to talk to my parents." She hurried away, hoping her friends would buy the lie. She liked Francisco and intended to say yes, but she didn't want them to know. Not yet. Not when it was the first date she'd have had in far too long.

Tapping out her reply, Natalie settled down in her room and decided that she liked using the glasses they had made to help the magical community. They were proving to be good for a lot of different elements of her life.

NOTE FROM RENÉE

APRIL 1, 2023

You made it to the middle book of the new series! Hope that means you're enjoying it. Thank you for reading the book and all the way back here to these notes.

For the last week, I have not done much writing. I was getting my house in order because Scotland loomed. Now I'm here, and it's lovely in its fog-shrouded glory! The seagulls greeted me at the house with a rousing chorus, and I saw the resident seals this morning. I am happy. I will have my first scone in a bit.

I had an uneventful pair of flights. For those who avail themselves of such things, which I do because I like the unlimited lattes and other goodies, I have now determined that Delta Sky Lounges are better than AmEx Centurion lounges. The food is better, the people are nicer, and most importantly, they have to-go cups for the (Starbucks) coffee! This won't excite many people, but I had the most fabulous sautéed Brussels sprouts at the JFK Delta Lounge. I actually went back for seconds, they were so good. They were vegan, too. Who'da thunk?

Got to Edinburgh at 10am after a night flight with only three hours of sleep and had to pick up my car from a new place. I carefully looked at the signs and headed in what I thought was the right direction to the NCP Scotpark shuttle, only to be told by a helpful bus driver (he asked if I "were a'reet." I must have looked confused), who directed me back the other way. When the shuttle bus came, they directed me back the first way. Oh, well. I needed the exercise after the flights, and my bags weren't TOO heavy, plus they had wheels.

If you haven't tried Virtuo in Europe (govirtuo.com), it's a great way to rent nice cars for much less than the going rate at the major agencies. They also have terrific insurance for about half what the majors sell it for. This time I have a BMW116i, which is spacious inside. I got it plus premium insurance for less than the price of a Vauxhall compact from Hertz, even the AAA rate, and I would have been relying on my credit card insurance if I had a problem (AmEx covers rental cars). When you travel as much as I do, you learn these things 😊

I have caught up with a few people, but mostly, I have been fighting jet lag, which I usually don't. Then again, I usually fly into Heathrow and drive for six hours, which makes me tired enough to sleep for twelve hours, and then I am on schedule. Darn that convenient and cheap flight I booked this time!

Exciting news! My friend Isabel Campbell, one of the people I visit in Scotland (although we haven't caught up in the last three days), just had two series accepted by LMBPN! I can't say much more now, but I'm very excited for her. More news in my next author notes, along with the blurb for the first series. We authors have to support each other, especially those who like scones and haggis.

As always, my profound thanks go to my advance readers and the proofreader team, the ones who read my stories after they are edited. They help make this book (and every book) its best. You are essential to my continued mental health. Thank you so much!

I hope you enjoyed the start of Natalie's, Steve's, and Mike's adventures so far. Tell me what you think in a review, please. Those keep us writers going! We are very grateful when a fan takes the time to do that for us and for the other people who might want to venture into this world.

Until next time,
Renée

BOOKS FROM RENÉE

Para-Military Recruiter
(with Michael Anderle)
Drafted (Book 1)
Recruiter (Book 2)
Accepted (Book 3)
Lead (Book 4)
Recruited (Book 5)
Soldier (Book 6)
Tactical (Book 7)

Piercing the Veil
Dangerous Opportunities (Book 1)
Dangerous Responsibilities (Book 2)
Decisions to Make (Book 3)

Reincarnation of the Morrigan
Birth of a Goddess (Book One)
The Way of Wisdom (Book Two)
Angelic Death (Book Three)

A Cold War (Book 4)
A Battle Tune (Book 5)
Broken Ice (Book 6)
A Torn Veil (Book 7)
Sins of the Past (Book 8)
The Wild Hunt Comes (Book 9)

The WereWitch Series
Bad Attitude (Book One)
A Bit Aggressive (Book Two)
Too Much Magic (Book Three)
Were War (Book Four)
Were Rages (Book Five)
God Ender (Book Six)
God Trials (Book Seven)
The Troll Solution (Book Eight)
Winner Takes All (Book Nine)

Callie Hart Series
Thin Ice (Book One)
Cold Blood (Book Two)
Feelings Run Deep (Book Three)

BOOKS BY MICHAEL ANDERLE

Sign up for the LMBPN email list to be notified of new releases and special deals!

https://lmbpn.com/email/

For a complete list of books by Michael Anderle, please visit:

www.lmbpn.com/ma-books/

Connect with Renée

Facebook: https://www.facebook.com/reneejaggerauthor

Website: https://reneejagger.com/

Connect with Michael Anderle

Website: http://lmbpn.com

Email List: https://michael.beehiiv.com/

https://www.facebook.com/LMBPNPublishing

https://twitter.com/MichaelAnderle

https://www.instagram.com/lmbpn_publishing/

https://www.bookbub.com/authors/michael-anderle